MW00977166

the power of
TWO

the power of
TWO

DR NII WALLACE-BRUCE

Anomalos Publishing House

Crane

HighWay
A division of Anomalos Publishing House, Crane 65633
© 2008 by Dr Nii Lante Wallace-Bruce
All rights reserved. Published 2008
Printed in the United States of America
08   1
ISBN-10: 0981509118 (paper)
EAN-13: 9780981509112 (paper)

Cover illustration and design by Steve Warner

All Bible quotations are from the New Living Translation unless
otherwise stated.

A CIP catalog record for this book is available from the Library of
Congress.

Contents

Part Two
The Power of Two in Practice

Acknowledgements

I wish to record my appreciation to all those who helped me in various ways. Specific mention is made of the following: Rose E. Aderolili, Nii Odartey Wallace-Bruce, Abraham Azubuike, Emmanuel Bartels-Kodwo, and Rebecca Nabwteme.

I also wish to thank my publishers for their great work. Special mention is made of Mr. Tom Horn, Ms. Donna Howell, Ms. Michelle Warner, Ms. Kelly Jo Eldredge, and the rest of the team at Anomalos.

With the Power of Two, You Can Rise to Greatness

Today is the beginning of the rest of your life.

—A COMMON SAYING

The future starts today, not tomorrow.

—POPE JOHN PAUL II

You desire to move on in life. You have ambitions. You want to make progress, rapid progress in life. But you cannot seem to pull it off. You take two steps forward, but then you soon take three steps backward. You are either back to the proverbial square one, or you end up just marginally ahead. Your life is stale and stalled, and you cannot understand why. There is no spring in your step. You are just managing to get through life, and your ambitions and big dreams never seem to be materializing.

Or worse, your life is in a rut. You are stuck, and you have no clue how to get out of the pit in which you find yourself. Your situation seems hopeless and helpless. You have experienced more days of depression and sadness than positive days. Life is just not meaningful to you. It is a permanent struggle, and sometimes the battle seems lost before you even start thinking of solutions.

Maybe you do not fit into the first two categories mentioned. Your life is actually not bad at all. Life has been fair and kind to you. You own that flashy four-wheel drive, BMW, Mercedes Benz, Porsche, Cadillac, or some other nice car. You have a big house and enjoy the comforts of life. Your life is not one of mediocrity. You already have a powerful and influential post. You may be a leader in the armed forces, in some other service organization, or in the community. You are somebody, and your life is going somewhere. You are well-connected and highly respected in your town. You are a mover and shaker in your city or even your country. You may even be a force to reckon with on the international scene. You have arrived, as they say!

But despite all these achievements, all these material comforts, all this power and influence, there is no peace and fulfillment in your life. At the end of all the great power plays of the day, you come home and feel miserable. You sip that expensive champagne or that rare whiskey, and you just gaze out the window, or your eyes simply follow the ripples in your swimming pool. Maybe staring into space is your style. It does not matter which method you adopt. You sit there and keep asking yourself, "Is that all there is in life?"

Your life is empty and unfulfilling. You have no peace. Money is not your problem. Power is not what you want now. You already have it in abundance. But you have no peace—no peace of mind. You lack fulfillment.

If you belong to any of these categories, this book is for you. This book is for people who want to achieve their destiny or mission in life. This book will show everyday people—ordinary people like you and me—how to progress in life and rise to greatness or superstar status. This book will show everyday, ordinary people how to rise to be great achievers, how to get out of the rut in which they have found themselves. This book is also for those who have average, mediocre lives but who desire to break the mold and rise to higher heights. This book will show people how to break the strongholds in their lives which are keeping them down and which are making them perpetually mediocre, average people.

Furthermore, this book will speak to people who are at the top of their tree, people who are successful in their professions, doctors, lawyers, engineers, financial experts, pastors, leaders of spiritual ministries, and all kinds of professionals, but who are wrestling with lack of fulfillment. This book is also for leading businessmen and businesswomen, community leaders, and leaders in the armed forces and in other service organizations. These are people who can afford all the material comforts of life but whose lives are miserable, because they are lacking the essential things which money cannot buy: peace and fulfillment. This book will show them how to obtain those essentials.

There is something for everyone in this book. It will set you free from whatever is plaguing you and holding you back. If you genuinely desire to breakthrough to greatness, superstar status, or be a significant achiever in some way, don't put this book down. Proceed to read it carefully and with enthusiasm. If you have already given up on life, and you do not want to break out of your situation, then put this book down and don't waste any more time. This book is not for losers or people who have given up on life. This book is for people who want to rise to greatness, superstar status, or become significant achievers in life. Above all, this book is for people who want to achieve their destiny or mission in life.

The Approach of the Book

This book seeks to challenge you to look at life from a completely new perspective: the power of two. The book will show you how the combination of two powers can lead you to greatness, superstar status, or some other significant achievement in life. In the following chapters, I will explain what the power of two is all about and why it is an entirely new perspective. The book is aimed to challenge you, to rock your world, to disturb and destabilize you, so that you will begin to shift from where you are now and approach life from this new perspective, the power of two. It is the aim of this book to take away your comfort zone, so that you will be shaken out of your slumber. It intends to make sleepers wake up and sit up. Let today be a new dawn in your life, and let this book be your life's companion on the way to your destiny.

The Purpose of the Book

This book's purpose is to give you a new perspective on life and to teach you the principles of the power of two, or the ultimate partnership.

The power of two will lead you to achieve your destiny or mission in life.

This book aims to catapult you into a new way of viewing and approaching life.

This book will offer peace and fulfillment to those seeking a new perspective on life.

PART ONE

||||||||||||||||||||||||||||||||||||||||||||||||||||||||||||||||||||||||||||||||||||||||||||||||||||||

introducing
the power of
TWO

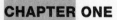

CHAPTER ONE

What is the Power of Two?

We work together as partners who belong to God.
You are God's field, God's building—not ours.

—1 Corinthians 3:9

The essence of the power of two is that in this life you need the combination of two powers to succeed. First, you need your own power, willpower, and self-belief. We all know that. We have heard it so many times. We have heard from motivation gurus, meditation teachers, life coaches, and many others that we have within us all that we need to make it in life. They teach that inside us dwells all that it takes to achieve our dreams and desires. We simply need to know how to harness it, how to bring that inner power into action to work for us. Some of us learned this from our teachers in school. We even learned some of it from our parents and peers.

Yes, there is a lot you can do on your own. There is a lot that you can achieve if you apply yourself and follow certain principles in life. You can make it far in life, indeed. That is why there is a legion of how to do–it–yourself books out there on just about any subject. Some of those books do not tell you much that you do not already know, but there is definitely a place for books on how to do things yourself.

However, the theme that will be resonating throughout this book is that the power of one, or your own power, is not sufficient to propel you to greatness, to superstar status, or to be a significant achiever in some way. What you need to be able to rise to these higher heights is the power of two. In order to rise above the pack and make it big in life, you need extra firepower. You need additional power. To be precise, you need something more powerful than yourself or your own willpower.

The power of two states that you need a power greater than your own to work with you. The two powers have to work in unity, not independently. I will explain in the succeeding sections of this chapter and the chapters following what exactly I mean by the power of one, the power of two, and how the latter in particular is meant to work in practice—how it can be applied to propel a person to greatness, superstar status, or to be a significant achiever in general.

First, There Was the Power of One

When I lived in Australia, a book came out in the 1990s which I enjoyed very much. It was titled The Power of One, by Bryce Courtenay, and it took the Australian book scene by storm. The book became a bestseller and was later made into a movie. I found it very powerful, because at that time of my life I believed in the power of one.

Bryce Courtenay's book is set in South Africa in the 1940s and 1950s. It is a story of a young, white, English boy who battled many obstacles in a country in which racial discrimination was deep and pervasive. In order to fight his way through such a system, he learned boxing.

In particular, he was taught the idea, "First, with the head and then with the heart, that's how a man stays ahead from the start." Using the combination of his genius, boxing skills, and tenacity, this English boy fought discrimination and injustice at every turn, and he ended up leading all the tribes of Africa.

What I loved about The Power of One was that it was full of inspiration. It taught how one determined person could take on a whole system and triumph. When I first read the book, I was captivated by it, and I re-read it several times. I have not read it for some years now, but I still remember the impact it had on me.

The term "the power of one" has since been employed by people in a variety of industries, such as the computer industry, to refer to various circumstances. However, the underlying point has not changed—one person or one material item can make a significant difference in life, business, or whatever the situation.

About the same time I read The Power of One, I came to know Frank Sinatra's famous song, I Did It My Way. That song was about how one man, in that case Frank Sinatra himself, did things his way. In the song, Sinatra sang that he had only a few regrets in leading his life the way he chose. He did it his way—he was in control of his own life, and he made his own choices. Looking back, he was generally happy with the choices and decisions he had made. His choices made him into a famous crooner, known around the world. Frank Sinatra was a clear example of the use of the power of one.

The point I wish to make from these two illustrations is that there is a place for what you and I can do on our own. Bryce Courtenay's book shows us how one determined person can virtually take on a whole system. For more than forty years this was my personal philosophy: I could do it. I could do anything. I believed in the power of one. I was convinced it worked, and I practiced it daily.

I practiced it when I was a university student. I also applied it when I was a lawyer in Australia with great success. When I became a university academic, I applied it again, and it continued to work well for me. I believed in the philosophy that I could do anything, and I was able to achieve much in my life. I had an above-average life. I was a successful university academic with a nice home and a nice car. I was doing fine.

I am sure that you can also attest to the power of one, either in your own life or in the lives of people you have come across who have created success by believing in themselves. You have witnessed the conviction, effort, ability, and determination that bring success. It is not hard to find such people. They are in every country, every town, every profession, every industry, and every organization. Self-made individuals and people who have struggled through life to get somewhere through determined efforts on their own part are not hard to come by.

There are numerous books written by or about such people. In one form or another, all those people practiced the power of one.

But more recently I have become wiser! I have come to learn that the power of one is insufficient. You need the power of two to achieve ultimate success and attain fulfillment in this life. You need the power of two to take you to your destiny. The power of one can take you far. It can help you achieve material things and status, but it is not adequate to take you to your destiny. To rise to greatness, superstar status, or to become a significant achiever in life, you need the power of two. It is the latter which will lead you to your mission in life.

Now Comes the Power of Two

We are that ultimate paradox, the finite made for the infinite. Anything less than God cannot satisfy our hunger for the divine. Not even success. That is why everything else, if we give it our ultimate loyalty—money, fame, drugs, sex, whatever— turns into ashes in our mouths.

—ARCHBISHOP DESMOND TUTU

What exactly is the power of two? It is the combination of two powers working together for your good. The power of two is the combination of your power of one and the additional firepower that you need to propel you along to your destiny. We have talked about your own power, your own abilities, efforts, and determination. That is the power of one. The extra firepower, the second power in the partnership, is a higher power—a power greater than your own.

Before you jump to the conclusion that this is nothing new, that many people already believe in the supernatural, let me explain the power of two more clearly. The power of two is not about believing in a supernatural being. It is not about simply believing in God and knowing about him. The power of two is not about a person possessing his or her own power and then believing in the existence of God or even knowing God. It is not about a person using the power of one and believing that there is a superior power up there somewhere. This is not what the power of two is about.

The power of two is also not about a person who believes in the power of one and applies it in daily life, but every now again, when the going gets tough, a higher power is called on for help, or specifically God is called on for assistance. That is why the concept behind this book is not called the powers of two, but rather the power of two.

To clarify the point, there are Christians who believe in God but conduct their daily lives more or less according to the power of one. They try to do things through their own efforts, abilities, and determination, while fervently believing in their God. As far as they are concerned, their God does not get involved in the daily details of life. However, their God is present when they need him. They can call upon him when they need him, and such people believe that their God will come to their aid at that time.

Perhaps the classic example of this is the behavior of the Israelites during the Exodus. From the time they were confronted with crossing the Red Sea all the way to arriving in the Promised Land, the vast majority of the Israelites did not rely totally on God. They knew God was there, but they tended to ignore him and do their own thing. However, in times of crisis, they looked to him for rescue. As a matter of fact, that very behavior of the Israelites continued and, as a consequence, ended in their captivity.

There are many people in the world today who hold similar beliefs—not just Christians. One may call this the dual approach: doing things substantially yourself but having a supernatural power in reserve that you can call upon when you need extra power. Here, we are talking about two powers operating independently from each other. It is up to the individual to decide if and when to call on the superior power, and it is up to the superior power whether to respond at all, and if so, when. As long as the person can get by without any big problems, there is no need to involve the supernatural, extra power. That power is kept in reserve to be used only when needed.

There are also people who do not believe in God or a higher power at all. For them, it is clear that they are relying solely on the power of one. Everything depends on them and them only. There is no reserve power.

However, the majority of people are likely to rely mostly on the power of one, but when things get sticky, they call upon God or another supernatural force to deploy extra firepower to help resolve whatever difficulty they may be facing. This tactic involves the use of two separate powers acting independently at different times. In such cases, the second power will be called upon only if the power of one is unable to resolve the problem at hand.

The power of two is not like that at all. The power of two is a combination of your power and that of your higher power. It is a partnership between you and your God in which the two powers work hand in hand. It is entirely different from a person relying on the power of one and then having a supernatural power in reserve to call upon in difficult circumstances.

What is advocated in this book is not the powers of two but rather the power of two. The power of two is a partnership between you and your God. I also call it the ultimate partnership. It is meant to operate in all aspects of your life and at all times. It does not involve two powers operating independently at different times. On the contrary, the power of two is meant to drive your life. It is this power of two which will lead you to achieve your mission in life. It is awesome. It offers a completely new approach, a new perspective. The power of two calls for a paradigm shift in your life. It calls for you to develop a new mindset. It defines a new path that will lead those who embrace it to their destiny.

I will discuss many examples of the power of two in operation as we go along, but let me give you two brief examples here.

In the Bible, we are told that when Jesus was calling his first disciples he met some fishermen on the shore of the Sea of Galilee. Jesus asked them to cast their nets into the water, but they were quite reluctant. Simon (also known as Peter) informed Jesus that they had worked hard all night, and they did not catch a single fish. But on the instructions of Jesus, they cast the nets into deeper waters, and bingo! There was such a huge catch that their nets began to tear (Luke 5:4–11).

Simon and his partners were experienced fishermen. They knew the tides; they knew the habitat of fish; they knew the behavior of fish; they also knew the right weather for fishing. They were experts in the techniques of trolling for fish. Indeed, they probably knew all that there was to know about fishing on the shore of the Sea of Galilee. All night they tried, but they did not catch anything.

That was the use of the power of one—their powers of one—each one of them. Based on their combined personal knowledge, skills, abilities, and experiences, they could not catch a thing. No human being could have done any better at that particular time. That explains why, when Jesus requested that they go back and cast their nets into the deeper waters, they were reluctant. They thought it was a waste of time. But they obeyed, simply because the instructions came from the Master. We now see the power of two coming into operation.

Once they followed the instructions of Jesus, there was extra power to find the fish—a divine power combined with their powers of one. In fact, the extra power Jesus supplied was so mighty that their nets overflowed with fish and began to break. With the power of one, they could catch nothing. But with the power of two, their success was beyond their wildest dreams.

The Bible records that their boats were so filled with fish that they were on the verge of sinking. That is the power of two! Simon Peter, his partners, and all the others who witnessed this incident were awestruck. But more significantly, for our purposes, that incident changed the destinies of Simon Peter and his partners. They literally dropped everything, kissed fishing goodbye, and immediately became Jesus's first disciples. They remained with Jesus to the very end and continued preaching the gospel long after his crucifixion and resurrection until their own deaths. That incident demonstrates clearly the difference between the power of one and the power of two. With the power of two, you will find your destiny or mission in life, and you will achieve it if you follow the principles set out in this book.

Another example I want to mention briefly here is that of Moses. (This will be discussed in greater detail in a later chapter.) The Bible tells us that Moses first tried on his own to liberate his people, the Israelites, from the bondage of the Egyptians. He tried to take the law into his own hands and fight the Egyptians, but he soon discovered that despite all the education and training he had received in Pharaoh's palace, he could not do so. As a result, he fled from Pharaoh's hands and into the desert (Exodus 2:11–15).

However, once God called and empowered him, it became an entirely different ballgame. Then the power of two was in operation. Moses had thought he could do it all through his own power, but he failed miserably. His power of one proved grossly inadequate. Indeed, he failed so miserably that he had to flee into the desert. Like Simon Peter, he tried hard but produced no results. His people still remained in slavery. Once Moses entered into an ultimate partnership with God, and their two powers were combined, they achieved their purpose of liberating the Israelites from the oppressive hands of Pharaoh. God achieved his mission, and through it Moses rose to greatness.

It should be noted here that once Moses and God entered into the ultimate partnership, Moses's destiny was changed forever. He changed from being a shepherd in the desert to a national leader, a spiritual leader, a liberator, and a hero. He went from being a lonely shepherd in the desert (in fact, a refugee), from somebody few people knew, to becoming so famous his reputation spread across the seas and the nations.

I also call the power of two the ultimate partnership, because it is a partnership between yourself and your God. It is the combination of your power and his power that will propel you to your destiny. This book will take you step by step through this new idea, this new concept, this new belief system. The book will take you through each principle of the ultimate partnership. But right now you may be asking yourself, why this partnership? Where does it come from?

The Basis of the Power of Two

We, without God, cannot; God without us, will not.
—St. Augustine of Hippo

Trust in the Lord with all your heart;
do not depend on your own understanding.
Seek his will in all you do,
and he will direct your paths.
—Proverbs 3:5–6

The basis of the power of two is that you are not on this earth by chance. You are on this earth because your God put you here. He put you on earth for a specific purpose, and it is his desire to work with you to achieve that purpose. You are not on this earth by some random act. God prepared for your life on earth, and the timing of your birth was planned far in advance. It was planned by your God so that you would achieve a specific purpose for him. In Ephesians 2:10 the Bible states, "For we are God's masterpiece. He has created us anew in Christ Jesus, so that we can do the good things he planned for us long ago."

Please don't believe what the scientists tell you. Scientists will have us believe that the universe came into being on its own. According to them, the universe came into being billions of years ago as a result of the big bang. Now some of the leading brains behind that theory are having second thoughts. For example, Sir Roger Penrose, a leading authority on the cosmos and the universe recently declared that he thinks the big bang theory is flawed. Throughout his career Sir Roger had advocated the big bang theory. Now he argues that there was not one big bang but a series of bangs. The fact of the matter is that scientists are not sure of how the universe came into being, but the Bible is certain that God created the earth and created human beings, starting with Adam and Eve.

In particular, you should not believe the theory, idea, or suggestion that you are on this earth because your father's spermatozoa was the fittest of them all, or that it was so athletic it was able to beat thousands of others to reach an embryo in your mother's womb, and you are the product. Even if that is how it happened, it so happened because your God planned it that way. He planned for you to enter this earth through your mother and father at the very time that you were born. The whole process had very little to do with the powers and abilities of your mother, your father, or for that matter yourself.

Of course, the same goes for me and for all other human beings. No human birth is accidental. It was planned by God, your own God, to happen at the time it did and in the manner in which it did. It was God's idea, and he wanted you to be on earth so that he would work with you to achieve a specific purpose. Therefore, it is very important for you to recognize that you are not on this earth as a statistic—a tiny spec of the world's population of 6.5 billion. You are also not on earth simply because your parents brought you into being. Rather, you are here because God created you through your parents so that he could work with you in a partnership. There is a definite purpose behind your being on earth. If you do not know this by now, it is my sincere hope that you realize it sooner, rather than later. It is not difficult to recognize that you have a purpose on earth. This book will help you find it.

The Con of Evolution

One of the greatest cons committed against humanity is the theory of evolution. Evolutionists would like us to believe that human beings evolved from apes. They cannot give us a reason why the human race began to evolve in the first place. They assume that it all just started by chance. This is nonsense! Something must have started it all. I believe that God created human beings. More specifically, he created each one of us for a specific purpose. That is why God needs to work with us in partnership to achieve that purpose.

The father of evolution Charles Darwin put forward his idea of natural selection and the survival of the fittest back in 1859 in his book, On the Origins of Species by Means of Natural Selection, or the Preservation of Favoured Races in the Struggle for Life. His theory has since formed the foundation of evolution in particular and biology in general. But this evolution thing has proved to be a big joke, the biggest joke ever played on the international community.

According to the evolutionists, we are on this earth completely by chance. We are aimless and purposeless. We got here because random animal life forms started to evolve. Charles Darwin and the other evolutionists would like us to believe that human beings evolved from apes and other animal life forms, that this evolution has been happening since the beginning of time, and more importantly, that it is continuing. The evolution theory holds that the process is continuing even to this day.

But where is the evidence to support evolution? Darwin published his book in 1859. After its publication, paleontologists, paleoanthropologists, paleoecologists, paleontologists, human biologists, anthropologists, archeologists, scientists, and other curious people began to roam the world frantically in search of evidence to back up the theory of evolution. For more than 100 years, they were unable to come up with any evidence to support Darwin's theory of evolution that human beings evolved from primates and other pre-human forms.

In November 1974, the world was told that there had been a breakthrough. American anthropologist, Donald Johanson, and his team dug up a fossil skeleton in the Afar Depression in Ethiopia. It was hailed as humankind's ancestor—the first concrete evidence needed to support the theory of evolution. This creature was given the scientific name Australopithecus afarensis. It was also nicknamed "Lucy" by Johanson and his team, because they celebrated the find with the famous Beatles song, Lucy in the Sky with Diamonds. The Ethiopians call the skeleton, Dinknesh, meaning "wonderful." But you have to see Lucy yourself to recognize that this so-called find is a big joke played on the whole international community.

Right now I am writing in Addis Ababa, the capital of Ethiopia. I have recently returned from the National Museum, where I have seen the original Lucy and a reconstructed version. I have observed it a few times now, and with every observation I come to the conclusion that

Lucy was just an ape, pure and simple. Lucy is no human being in any shape or form. The scientists would like us to believe that Lucy was the earliest form of humans, but the fact still remains that Lucy was an ape and nothing more than that.

To start with, the fossil skeleton of Lucy is only 40 percent complete. In particular, the skull is so incomplete that it is very difficult to study or observe it carefully for purposes of comparison. How can scientists seriously come to a conclusion based on only 40 percent of the evidence? They claim that Lucy is the most complete hominid ever found, but the thing is only 40 percent intact. In most countries, a legal case has to be proved either on a balance of probabilities (if it is a civil case) or beyond a reasonable doubt in criminal cases. In the United States, the balance of probabilities is called the preponderance of evidence, which means that the evidence should be greater than 50 percent. Hence, the evidence that scientists have in Lucy does not even meet this lower standard of proof.

Those who discovered Lucy placed her in the human family, because it looked like she walked upright. But why would animals that were walking on all fours suddenly want to walk upright? Why? It just happened? I don't believe so, and the scientists cannot provide a persuasive explanation for this sudden evolution.

Lucy is said to have a small ape-like brain and other features similar to a chimpanzee. Is that evidence of evolution? I have seen this Lucy thing with my own naked eyes. There is hardly anything to identify it as human, even if the scientists insist it is a pre-human form. The thing in the Ethiopian National Museum is simply an ape, or to be more precise, the skeletal remains of an ape. That is all there is to it.

Let the truth be told, the scientific community, especially the evolutionists, were desperate to find evidence of a link between human beings, animals, and other pre-human life forms. They were desperate after finding nothing more than 100 years after the publication of Darwin's book. So they settled on Dinknesh and gave it a scientific name.

It is significant to note that no fossil skeleton has been found since Lucy to show us Lucy's family or generation. Other fossils have been found in Ethiopia, Kenya, Chad, Tanzania, and South Africa, but nothing has been found that is more convincing than Lucy. How come? Many questions remain unanswered. Darwin published his book in 1859. Today, we have the most advanced technology, research, and investigation techniques ever known to humankind. Yet to this day the best evidence that the evolutionists can come up with is Lucy, a lonely, pathetic, partial, female ape that lived some 3.5 million years ago in the Afar Depression of Ethiopia. Did Lucy live on this earth by herself? If she did evolve as we are told, did Lucy evolve alone? If not, where are her siblings and other relatives?

Another big flaw in the whole evolution argument is that if Lucy represents one of the earliest forms of human life, what happened to all those who evolved after her? What happened to the generation after Lucy, call it the "Mary" generation? What happened to the generation after that, call it the "Victoria" generation? Next there should have come another generation. Perhaps we can call it the "Elizabeth" generation. According to the evolutionists, it should go on and on and on until we get to the generation in which Charles Darwin was born. Where are all the generations between Lucy and Charles Darwin? Did they disappear? By way of contrast, the Bible has been able to record the genealogy from Adam onwards, all the way to Jesus Christ.

There is another gaping hole in the evolution theory. If today scientists can find dinosaur fossils dating back many millions of years, why can't they find fossils dating back a meager four million years or even less? If they can find fossils for dinosaurs, why can't they find them for hominids? The answer is simple—there isn't any evidence to prove that human beings evolved from apes or other animal life forms.

An additional point is the claim that human beings just randomly began life on earth and evolved, a purposeless existence. This point is not convincing. The whole idea that human beings spontaneously evolved from animals and other life forms because of the survival of the fittest or natural selection has no solid foundation. It is a fictional scenario that developed in Charles Darwin's mind and the minds of his associates. It is not based on solid evidence that can be independently verified by other scientists.

Speaking for myself, I have been to the Ethiopian National Museum a few times to study and observe this thing they call Lucy. It is just an ape, and it is an insult to all humankind to say that we evolved from that thing or something like it.

Coming Back to the Power of Two

Do you realize that you are God's partner?
—Archbishop Desmond Tutu

Having debunked the theory that human beings spontaneously evolved on earth, and that there is no particular purpose to their existence, let us return to the power of two. It states that human beings were created by God. Each one of us was created by God. God created you and me, and he did so for a purpose. In the Bible, God himself says, "I knew you before I formed you in your mother's womb. Before you were born I set you apart" (Jeremiah 1:5).

We are not on earth just because we evolved, but equally important, we are not on earth to roam around the planet without any particular purpose or aim. On the contrary, God made each one of us with a purpose in mind. In order to achieve that purpose, he needs to work with us in partnership. This is what I call the ultimate partnership. Each one of us is so unique that we could only have been made intelligently and deliberately by God for the specific purpose he had in mind.

You were born to your parents in a particular town and country, but location is easy to change. God simply used your parents as the entry point for your arrival on earth. You can change your nationality and residence if you choose. So where you were born is nothing immutable or especially significant. You probably know many people who have changed their nationalities or taken on an additional nationality. Similarly, there are many people who have moved away from the original place where they were born.

You can also change the name your parents gave you at birth and take on a name of your own choice. Again, there are many people who have changed all or part of their birth name. Some people became

famous using nicknames, assumed names, or names different from what
their parents gave them at birth. The general public would not recognize
their original names. Examples can easily be found in the sports world
and in the entertainment industry. Bono of the famous Irish rock band
U2 is a classic. His real name is Paul Hewson, but few people remember
the name given to him by his parents. I had to go on to the web and do
some research to find it myself. Bono is influential today on the world
stage. He meets presidents, prime ministers, and other heads of state.
He rubs shoulders with leading business people and community leaders. Wherever he goes, he is known by the single name Bono. I would
assume few people, if any, call him by the name given to him at birth.

As you mature in life, you will have less and less to do with your
parents. It is part of the growing-up process. We are meant to develop
that way. It is the same way in which your parents developed. So
the point of all this is that as you mature, you can easily change the
things you received from your parents at birth, especially nationality,
residence, and name. However, you cannot change the things your creator gave you when he made you. You cannot change your DNA. You
cannot change your genetic makeup. You cannot change your finger-
prints, voiceprint, or footprints. You cannot change your race or skin
color. These are the things which truly make you unique. A person
may resemble you, particularly a relative, but certain characteristics are
unique to you only. That is what makes you, you. On the entire globe,
there is not one other person who is an exact match. There is no clone
of you anywhere, because your maker created an original.

Equally important, your maker put inside you certain traits which
are also unique. They constitute your inner self. This power inside you
is the source of your power of one. It is through your inner self that
your creator can influence your life. Your God can communicate with
you, and you can maintain a partnership with him.

Why does God need you? The power of two teaches that you should
see the second or supernatural power as your very own. Yes, the power
of two teaches that God sees you as an individual, and you should see
him as your personal God. God made you a unique person and gave
you unique attributes for a specific purpose. You should also see him as

unique to you, your own God, to work with in partnership.

If you are a Christian, you believe that there is one God for all Christian believers. The power of two teaches that you should not see him as far away from you, or busy working on the problems of other believers, or dismissing you as an insignificant member of his kingdom. You should not see God far removed from you and sitting on his throne in the heavens waiting for you to make contact with him. The power of two teaches that you should embrace God as your own. He is your creator, your maker. He is your father, and even though he may be there for others as well, many others in fact, you should treat him in the same way as he treats you. He treats you as a distinct person with a mission to fulfill. Therefore, you should also embrace him and deal with him on a personal level. He is yours, just as you are his. This is a fundamental element of the power of two.

It does not matter what your religion or denomination. Your God is unique to you. The fact that millions or even billions believe in that same God is not the point. Yours is not a God of millions or billions. He is your God. The fact that you sometimes pray in fellowship with others, in a prayer group or in the church, does not change your relationship with God. Each one of you prays to your own God. You are praying or worshipping corporately, but the prayer is personal. He is your personal God, whether you are alone or in a group.

Now back to the question, why does God need you at all? After all, he is omnipresent, omnipotent, omniscient, and sovereign. He created the world and created you. He is so powerful and awesome that he can breathe things into existence. He can speak things into existence, and he can also speak them out of existence. He can make things happen at any time; he can turn the impossible into the possible. He has all the resources of the universe at his disposal. There is no restriction or restraint on what God can do. You are just one person, one little human being, struggling with the challenges of daily life. So why would God need you?

1984 Nobel Peace Prize winner and Archbishop Emeritus of Cape Town, Desmond Tutu, discusses at length in his book, *God Has a Dream, a Vision of Hope for our Time*, why God desires to work with us.

In short, God needs partners on earth to achieve his purposes. Not our purposes, his purposes. The individual missions God assigns to us are part of his elaborate plan on earth. So your mission and my mission are simply pieces of God's mighty jigsaw puzzle.

The Bible teaches us that throughout history God has worked through human beings. On some rare occasions, God worked through animals, like when he made a donkey speak with a human voice (Numbers 22:28–30). This was an exception, presumably because God could not get a human being to carry out that particular task. The norm is that God has worked through human beings since the creation of the earth. Some significant illustrations will serve to buttress the point here.

When God wanted to liberate the Israelites from Egypt, he approached Moses on the edge of the desert in the burning bush. God worked through Moses and his brother Aaron to get the Israelites out of Egypt. Throughout the forty years that there were in the wilderness, God worked through Moses, directing him on what to do and what to say to the Israelites. When Moses died, God turned to Joshua to lead his people to the Promised Land.

Another illustration is when God wanted to liberate his people from the torment of the Midianites. He did not start a war himself. He chose Gideon and instructed him on the number of people needed for the battle and also the military strategy that should be adopted. God worked through this man to achieve a great victory for his people (Judges 6).

Yet another powerful illustration is when God decided to send a savior to come down to earth and save his people. He did not do it from his throne in heaven. The Israelites did not wake up one day and find someone in white robes in the sky claiming that he had been sent from heaven to deliver God's people. That person would have been stoned to death instantly. Nor did God cause thunder and lightening to crisscross the sky, and then when the whole world was watching, drop an angel from the heavens to save his people. Rather, God worked through human beings.

First, God chose Mary, an innocent virgin in a tiny village, for the purpose. Joseph, the husband of Mary, was visited by angels who explained God's plan to him. He understood and kept his wife, though he was not the father of the child in her womb. God used two human beings to bring his own son into the world.

Do you remember Jonah? God chose him to go and preach to the people of Nineveh and warn them to change their ways. What did Jonah do? First he gave excuses, and then he ran away. But Nineveh was his assignment. That was his purpose on this earth, and because the project was very important to God, Jonah was not allowed to escape. Even when he was swallowed by the great fish, God made sure that he was not eaten up. God kept him alive and delivered him out of the mouth of that great fish. Through Jonah, God delivered the people of Nineveh.

There are numerous other examples throughout the Bible of how God worked through human beings. God appointed various human beings as his prophets or spokespersons. Even God's word, as contained in the Bible, was written by human beings. God inspired them to write it—God anointed particular people to write his word for all (2 Timothy 3:16).

This is how God still works today. Working through humans is his first preference. He made human beings, and so he prefers to work with them and through them. Therefore, God needs you. He needs you to achieve the specific purpose for which he brought you into this life. He is the only person who knows why he created you. In the Bible, God tells us, "I knew you before I formed you in your mother's womb. Before you were born I set you apart and appointed you" (Jeremiah 1:5).

In that particular scripture, God said he appointed Jeremiah, even before he was born, to be his spokesman to the world. The same applies to you and me. God has a specific mission for us. He planned it long before we were even born. Once we are on earth, he will activate the mission and bring it to fruition. Through your inner self, God lets you know why he made you. He reveals your purpose, your mission in this life. If you don't know what it is yet, God will gladly tell you.

But you have to be in a partnership with God first. You need to have an intimate relationship with him. God may also use you to help someone else get onto his or her path. Once you are in a partnership with God, you will know your mission. Your destiny may be intertwined with other people. Whatever it is, God needs you. He does not like to do things by himself. He prefers to work with you, and there are numerous examples of this in the Bible, both in the Old and New Testament. God works in the same way today. He has not changed. He still wants to join you in the ultimate partnership to achieve his purpose and your destiny on this earth. It is for this purpose that he brought you into being.

Summary

What the power of two is all about is that in this world you need a combination of two powers to be able to rise to greatness, superstar status, or significant achievement. You need the power of two to attain ultimate fulfillment in this life.

There is no doubt about the fact that you can achieve a lot by yourself. Through your own efforts, your own abilities, willpower, determination, and tenacity you can achieve a lot for yourself. That applies to life in general, but it also applies to particular aspects of life, such as in marriage, finances, children, career, business, ministry, and community work. There is a lot that you can achieve all by yourself. That is the power of one.

However, as this book will show you, the power of one is insufficient to propel you to greatness. You may be at the top of your profession. You may be up there with the top business men and women, the captains of industry, leaders in the armed forces or other service organizations. You may have your own ministry as a pastor or a worship leader in a church. If you are only using the power of one, you will still be left with a strong, nagging feeling that there is something missing in your life.

You may have all the comforts of this life. You may have all material things at your beck and call. You may be quite influential in your town, city, or country. You may even be influential on the global scene. You may be a mover and shaker in the corridors of power. Yet despite all the outward appearances of success, you may be in turmoil inside. There may be a yawning gap inside you in spite of the material success surrounding you. You may even be slowly and quietly whittling away inside. You may be wondering what is wrong with you, or you may even be saying aloud that there is something missing in your life. You may lose sleep at night. Perhaps you just sit up most nights and cry—not even knowing what you are crying about.

Believe me, you are not alone. There are many, many people just like you. The explanation is that the power of one is inadequate to give you completeness or fulfillment in this life.

The power of two supplies the missing link. The power of two states that you need another power to make you complete. This extra power, higher power, is a supernatural power. It is a divine power. You need it to work in combination with your own power of one. This power belongs to God.

The power of two is not about you having your power of one and then having a supernatural power in reserve to call upon in difficult times. That approach relies on two separate powers which operate independently and at different times. Many Christians take that approach. They rely on their power of one in day-to-day living, but when crisis comes they call upon God for help. They call upon the supernatural power if and only if their power of one is unable to deliver. This may be true with followers of other religions, as well. By doing this, they make their higher power a god of crisis management.

Instead, the power of two is about you having an intimate relationship with God, your God, and then combining his power with your own to achieve his mission for you in this life.

In Part 2 of this book I will show you just how the power of two works and how you can use its principles to propel you to your destiny. In order to ground the discussion in actual historical and practical examples, let us first look at some people who were destined for greatness but messed up. We will start by learning from them.

Power 2 Principles

The power of two states that you should combine your power of one with the extra firepower of a higher power. You need to work in partnership with God, not separately and when it is convenient.

With the power of two, God is able to achieve the purpose for which he created you, and you are able to achieve your destiny on this earth. It is this ultimate partnership that will propel you to greatness, superstar status, or significant achievement.

CHAPTER TWO

People Destined for Greatness Who Messed Up Big Time

I said to myself, "Come now, let's give pleasure a try.
Let's look for the `good things' in life."
But I found that this, too, was meaningless.

—ECCLESIASTES 2:1

And this, too, is a very serious problem.
As people come into this world, so they depart.
All their hard work is for nothing.
They have been working for the wind,
and everything will be swept away.
Throughout their lives, they live under a cloud —
frustrated, discouraged, and angry.

—ECCLESIASTES 5:16–17

In this chapter we will discuss the cases of some people who were destined for greatness or superstar status but messed up. They messed up enough to destroy their own destinies. The mess created by the first two examples, in fact, changed the course of history. We may describe these people as mega-messers.

We will look at four case studies in this chapter, two from biblical times and the other two from contemporary times. The purpose of these case studies is to demonstrate how the power of two works or does not work. We will learn some important lessons from them, and they will get us ready to fully digest how the power of two works in practice and, more importantly, how it can work for you and propel you to your destiny.

Learning from History

The Case of Great Grandpa Adam

According to the Bible, Adam was the first human being created by God. God created Adam from the dust of the earth with his own hands and breathed life into him. Adam was destined for greatness. He was destined to be the father of all humankind, not merely by being the first, but also through the anointing of God. Adam was given the privilege of living in the Garden of Eden and taking care of it. Adam was given the honor and authority to name all the animals and birds created by God.

Today your household pet is called a dog, cat, or parrot because Adam gave it that name. The names of all the birds, goats, sheep, cows, pigs, etc., on the farm were given by Adam. So are the names of the animals in the wild—the lions, elephants, and giraffes. It was also Adam who coined the word, "woman" (Genesis 2:23).

Adam was indeed destined for greatness. He had great wisdom. He had the rare privilege of taking walks in the Garden of Eden with God at sunset. One can imagine the two of them walking together, admiring the lushness of the garden, the beauty of the flowers and plants, and the pristine environment in general. They adored and admired the paradise of the garden and chatted while enjoying the freshness of the air. It was a wonderful partnership between God and the first man.

But then what happened? Adam messed up big time. He ate the forbidden fruit. God told him that he was entitled to eat every fruit in the garden with the exception of one. The instruction was given specifically and directly to him. God told Adam that he could fully enjoy the Garden of Eden. There were no restrictions on him except one. God left no doubt about this one rule. He commanded Adam to never eat fruit from the tree at the center of the garden. It was the tree of the knowledge of good and evil. God's warning was quite stern.

But what did Adam do? He ate the fruit and then blamed everyone else. God was swift in his punishment. He banished Adam and his wife from the Garden of Eden and pronounced judgment on both of them (Genesis 3:14–24). Today we are still suffering the effects of the punishment meted out by God to Adam and Eve.

What is the relevance of Great Grandpa Adam's story to the power of two? Adam was the first person created. We all came from him. That makes him our great, great, great...grandpa. Until the Fall (when Adam and his wife ate the forbidden fruit and lost favor with God), Great Grandpa Adam was destined for greatness. Up to that point he was living his life according to the principles of the power of two. There was an active partnership between Adam and God. They discussed things together; they took walks together in the Garden of Eden; they generally worked together; they had some shared responsibilities.

This was the first example of the ultimate partnership. God was concerned about Adam and the fact that he was lonely. Therefore God created a companion, Eve. As we have already seen, God gave Adam important responsibilities in the Garden of Eden. The partnership was working beautifully and as intended, until Adam chose to listen to his wife and disobeyed God. This turned out to be an error in judgment of monumental proportions. God was angry, very angry with Adam.

I do not understand Great Grandpa Adam. All he had to do was to stay away from one tree and its fruit in a majestic paradise. Great Grandpa Adam, I wish you could communicate with us from wherever you are now. Why was it difficult for you? You just had to keep away from the fruit of one tree, and you messed up. You were not forced or pressured by your wife to eat the fruit. She did not insist that it would give you peace of mind that day. Indeed, Eve did not make any demands. None at all. She simply offered it to you, and you disobeyed the command of your creator, the person who placed you in the garden, by eating it. Why, Great Grandpa? Why? Today we are still suffering the consequences of your actions.

We learn the following lessons from Great Grandpa Adam. First, until the Fall, Adam and God were operating on the power of two. It was the first ever partnership between a human being and the Creator. Everything was going wonderfully in that majestic garden.

The second lesson we learn is that when one of the partners violates the terms of the partnership, it is broken, and it may come to an end. In this case, Great Grandpa Adam did not keep his side of the bargain. He disobeyed God, and as a result God terminated the partnership. Thereafter, Adam was on his own—he had only the power of one. Yes, he could still survive, but he became severely limited in what he could do. His act of disobedience by eating the forbidden fruit led to the termination of the partnership. Once that happened, the power of two was at an end; Adam was left with his power of one.

We know from biblical accounts that after the Fall Adam lost his place of honor in the history of humankind. God had intended him to be the greatest of his creations, the father of all humankind, and the father of all nations. But after he broke the partnership and was banished from the Garden of Eden, he lost that unique privilege. He became less and less significant, until finally he faded away.

Adam was the first human being to be created, but he was not the father of all nations. That honor was bestowed upon Abraham. It was Abraham who operated on a power of two with God from when he was called until his death. It was Abraham whom God gave the rare honor of becoming the father of all nations. In Hebrews 11, persons of great faith are listed. It is a list of people to whom God gave his approval because of their confidence in him. Great Grandpa Adam is not mentioned. Abraham, of course, gets more than a passing reference. Even Rahab, the prostitute, gets a mention as a person of great stature when it comes to faith in God. The scriptural passage lists people who made a difference in the world—people who rose to greatness, superstar status, or were significant achievers one way or another.

And Great Grandpa Adam? Poor man, he was ignored, treated with the contempt that he deserved. The story of Great Grandpa Adam illustrates clearly how the power of two should operate and what will happen when it does not.

The Rise and Fall of King Saul

Saul was the first person to be anointed king of the Israelites. In the Bible, he was described as the tallest and most handsome man in Israel

(1 Samuel 9:2). Apart from this, he had no claim to fame. He was from the tribe of Benjamin, the smallest tribe in Israel, and in his own words his family was the least important within that tribe. His vocation was as a farmer. He helped his father and looked after the livestock.

God chose Saul to be the first king of Israel. God's prophet Samuel anointed him, and the people of Israel crowned him their king. Saul was made king when he was thirty years old, and for some time he was a successful king, winning many military victories. He became king at a time when the Israelites knew no peace. They were frequently attacked by their neighbors. But Saul brought them stability and a measure of peace. He fought and defeated Israel's enemies from all directions.

King Saul defeated Moab, Ammon, Edom, Zobah, the Philistines, and the Amalekites. It should be noted that battles were not simple affairs. Those were days of constant warfare and struggle for territory and the spoils of war. It was true survival of the fittest. The rule at that time was the strongest and most successful in battle reigned supreme. In other words, King Saul could have fought his neighbors not once but a few times, and he remained successful in keeping them at bay.

During that period, King Saul worked in partnership with God. However, he later disobeyed God, and God rejected him. Saul lived out the remainder of his life in torment and depression. In the end, he died a painful death at the hands of his archenemies, the Philistines. It was written of Saul and his son, "How the mighty heroes have fallen! Stripped of their weapons, they lie dead" (2 Samuel 1:27).

Beautifully put. Once God rejected him and took away his anointed power, Saul was finished.

How is King Saul relevant to the power of two? It demonstrates clearly how the power of two should work in practice. The case also teaches how the power of two should not be applied. When God chose Saul to become king, he was nobody. He was helping his father on the farm. He had no knowledge or experience of leadership or holding public office. In fact, other than his good looks, he had no claim to fame. Only God knew his purpose.

Once chosen, Saul was destined for greatness. His life was never to be the same again. He went from looking after his father's flock and tending the soil to being singled out by God for prominence. He was going to be the first king of Israel and much more. When God's prophet Samuel first met Saul, he said, "And I am here to tell you that you and your family are the focus of all Israel's hopes" (1 Samuel 9:19).

Saul was so shocked by what he heard that he found it necessary to tell Samuel he was talking to the wrong person. Saul said that he was not worthy—he was simply not the type of person Samuel had in mind. All of Israel's hopes would be placed on his shoulders? No, Saul did not think he could possibly be the right man for the job. He thought that it was a case of mistaken identity—a mistake on the part of Samuel.

But that is how God works. His ways are not our ways, and his decisions may not make sense to us. However, God appreciated that he had to equip Saul for such a high office. Saul was anointed by God's prophet, Samuel. As a result, the Spirit of the Lord descended and empowered Saul. To demonstrate his new influence Saul, who until then was a common farmer, was now able to prophesy. After his transformation, Saul was "changed into a different person" (1 Samuel 10:6). God was with him. In addition, God anointed a group of advisors for Saul in his home town (1 Samuel 10:26). God also changed Saul's heart.

So the first lesson we learn from the story of King Saul is that God chose an everyday person, an ordinary person, and destined him for greatness. He was not equipped for the mission on his own, but God gave him the power he needed.

The second lesson we learn from this case study is that God set out the terms and conditions of the partnership. Once Saul was chosen and empowered for the position, God did not leave him to struggle on his own. God was with him, but at the same time God did not give him the position and power without responsibilities. Saul was not given carte blanche. Instead, Samuel set out the terms and conditions of the appointment.

When Saul was formally named king, it was before all of Israel and all the tribal leaders. Unlike his anointing, this was a very public crowning at Mizpah. Saul was so humbled, in fact, so frightened, that he went into hiding. But the Lord revealed his hiding place, and he was crowned king of Israel in the presence of all. The important point here is that in the presence of all the people of Israel Samuel specified the rights and duties of the king. He even proceeded to write them down on a scroll and placed them before the Lord (1 Samuel 10:25). In other words, the terms and conditions of Saul's partnership with God were clearly spelled out and made public. The relationship between Saul and the people he was to govern was outlined in a similar fashion. The people of Israel were witnesses to these declarations.

The third lesson from this case study is that King Saul violated the terms of the partnership with God, and eventually God terminated their relationship. Saul started out very well. He listened to and obeyed God. He worked together with God through his earthly representative, the prophet Samuel. As we have already noted, Saul was successful and scored many major military victories for his people. But then it went into his head. He began to disconnect or disengage from God and to do his own thing. He disobeyed God more than once. He violated the terms of the partnership agreement with God. Instead of the power of two, he relied on the power of one.

As the story reveals, Saul was just an everyday person. He had no special qualities and was not equipped for leadership. But once God chose him, God empowered him. He was equipped appropriately for the position, and more importantly, God remained with him. When God empowered Saul, the power of two came into operation.

Without God, Saul could not do much. Even when he had been empowered, he felt so weak at his knees at his coronation that he went into hiding. There is no doubt that it was the power of two that got him started and kept him going. But once King Saul broke the terms of the partnership, he reverted to the power of one. He tried to do things his way, and he fell from God's favor. Like Grandpa Adam, King Saul messed up. He messed up big time.

King Saul's first breach of the partnership was at Gilgal. He was leading his people in a war against the Philistines. God, through Samuel, had instructed King Saul to wait seven days for Samuel to arrive. King Saul waited and waited, but Samuel did not arrive. Meanwhile, the

Philistines had amassed a huge and mighty army. So huge was their army that they had "as many warriors as the grains of sand along the seashore" (1 Samuel 13:5).

Then the Philistine army began to intimidate the Israelite troops, who started to lose their nerve. According to the Bible, the Israelite troops were trembling with fear, and there was mass desertion on the frontlines. King Saul started to panic. His instruction was to wait for Samuel to arrive no matter what. Put another way, King Saul was not to engage in battle before the arrival of the prophet Samuel.

To his credit, King Saul waited until the seventh day, but the Philistines were ready for battle and taunted and intimidated his troops. He began to lose his patience as he saw his troop strength dwindle. Saul continued to wait, but Samuel did not turn up. Eventually, Saul lost his patience and self-control and decided to offer sacrifices to the Lord himself (an essential act before war) so that he could engage the Philistines in battle. But just as Saul commenced to offer the sacrifices, Samuel emerged from the bushes.

It was too late. It was a matter of minutes, but nevertheless, King Saul had violated an essential term of the partnership agreement. He had done something reserved only for God's representative on earth. It was a serious act of disobedience. The prophet Samuel described King Saul's act as foolish. God was swift in pronouncing judgment:

> You have disobeyed the command of the Lord your God. Had you obeyed, the Lord would have established your kingdom over Israel forever. But now your dynasty must end, for the Lord has sought out a man after his own heart. The Lord has already chosen him to be king over his people, for you have not obeyed the Lord's command.
>
> —I SAMUEL 13:13–14

A significant aspect of this case is that God's judgment against King Saul related to the future of Saul's dynasty. God did not proceed to terminate the partnership immediately. He did not disempower

King Saul at that moment. God continued to be with him despite his disappointment with him. As a matter of fact, King Saul went on to win that particular battle against the Philistines, with his son Jonathan playing a leading role.

King Saul went on to score additional military victories against Israel's enemies. But then, he messed up again. He did not learn from the first mistake. He disobeyed God again. King Saul was sent on a mission against the Amalekites with clear instructions from God. King Saul chose not to carry out the instructions. When he was confronted by the prophet Samuel, he began to give excuses. But this time in God's eyes King Saul had gone too far. God was finished with him. The power of two was over between them. God pronounced his judgment:

> What is more pleasing to the Lord: your burnt offerings and sacrifices or your obedience to his voice? Obedience is far better than sacrifice.
>
> —1 SAMUEL 15:22

So as a consequence of this second act of disobedience, God rejected Saul. This time, God rejected him as king and disempowered him. The Bible says that the Spirit of the Lord left him. The lesson we draw from this is that the power of two came to an end. God terminated the partnership and abandoned Saul to his own devices. Saul was left with the path he had chosen for himself—to do things his own way. The power of one was all that remained.

We can see from this case study that Saul was destined for greatness. He was chosen by God to work with him in partnership. God's representative on earth was the prophet Samuel. Saul was to lead the people of Israel. God did not choose any of the existing leaders of the tribes of Israel. Instead, he singled out Saul for greatness and equipped him appropriately for the office of king. The terms and conditions of that partnership were set out publicly for all to witness.

Saul started very well, but through acts of disobedience he violated the partnership, and God terminated it. Saul had the opportunity to rise to greatness, but he messed up. He messed up big time. Once he no longer abided by the power of two, he lost his way. He was finished. Saul lost a rare opportunity to have his dynasty rule Israel forever.

If Saul had not messed up, his son Jonathan would have been the next king. But rather, the crown went to David. If Saul had not messed up and reverted to the power of one, it is probable that Jesus would have descended from his line. The course of history of the Israelites would have been different. Indeed, the history of the world would have been entirely different.

But what happened? Jesus came from King David's line. Saul and three of his sons perished on the same day, and then the name of his family just disappeared from history. Just like Great Grandpa Adam, Saul is not mentioned in Hebrews 11, where the prominent and faithful Israelites are listed. King Saul's rise demonstrates how the power of two works, and his fall demonstrates how it does not work.

Some Contemporary Examples

The Baddest Man on the Planet

He was born on June 30, 1966 in Brooklyn, New York. He had a troubled youth and spent time in juvenile detention centers. His potential as a fighter was recognized, and as a result he was taken out of reform school and given training in boxing. He had an impressive amateur career but narrowly failed to qualify to represent the United States in the Los Angeles Olympic Games in 1984. So he turned professional. He made his professional debut on March 6, 1985 in Albany, New York. He won by a knockout in the very first round. He fought frequently from that time on, and he won all his fights, most of them by a knockout in the first round.

On November 22, 1986, he won a second round knockout victory and became the WBC heavyweight champion of the world. He was only twenty years old and thus became the youngest ever heavyweight champion of the world.

His name is Michael Gerard Tyson. He has also been known as "Iron Mike" and "The Baddest Man on the Planet." Iron Mike took

the boxing world and the sports world in general by storm. He captivated fans and attracted a huge media interest. In 1987, he captured
the WBA and IBF world heavyweight titles in addition to the one he
already held. Thus, he became the undisputed heavyweight champion
of the world.

Tyson's impressive winning streak continued. In January 1988, he
dispatched the great former world champion, Larry Holmes, to the
canvas in the fourth round. Later that year Tyson knocked out Michael
Spinks, the former IBF world heavyweight champion, a mere ninety-
one seconds into the first round. Tyson seemed invincible, and he was
destroying his opponents with devastating predictability. The sporting
world loved him. He was an industry in his own right.

However, in February 1990 Tyson suffered his first defeat. He was
knocked out by lowly regarded James "Buster" Douglas in Tokyo in the
tenth round. As a consequence, Tyson lost all championship belts. Iron
Mike tried to stage a comeback, and in 1991 he seemed to be regaining
his former self. However, in 1992 he was sent to prison for rape. He
spent three years there. Upon release from prison, Tyson successfully
staged a comeback. In 1996 he won two of the world heavyweight title
belts he had lost back in 1990. But in November of 1996 Tyson was
defeated by Evander Holyfield.

Mike Tyson ended up in prison again in 1997 and served nine
months for assault. He tried to stage another comeback, but he never
regained any of the heavyweight championship belts. Between 2003
and 2005 he suffered terrible defeats—the last two at the hands of boxers who were considered to be, in boxing terms, "journeymen."

What is the relevance of the story of the Baddest Man on the Planet
to the power of two? Mike Tyson was destined for superstar status. No
one doubts that Iron Mike in fact achieved greatness. He became a
superstar. During his prime he was the most feared boxer in the world,
and he attracted huge media attention. People with little or no interest
in boxing even liked to watch Mike Tyson in action during his prime.

What happened to Iron Mike? He became the youngest world
heavyweight champion at age twenty. He became the undisputed
heavyweight champion of the world after being in the professional

sport for just over two years. At the time, Mike Tyson was considered to be the greatest boxer of his era, and many predicted that he would be the greatest boxer of all time. But that did not happen. Sure, Mike Tyson will remain on record as one of the greatest boxers of the twentieth century, but that is where his fame ends. Tyson's reign was short, too short. He did not even come close to dethroning Mohammed Ali as the greatest boxer of our time. Some say that Mohammed Ali was the greatest overall sports personality of the twentieth century, not just in the boxing world.

As far as the power of two is concerned, Tyson did not apply it. It would seem that Iron Mike only had the power of one. What made him so fearsome in the ring was that he had punching power like dynamite, speed, excellent head movement, stamina, and very good conditioning. He combined his skill with a unique psychological aspect. There was an aura of invincibility about him. He was so intimidating that many of his opponents suffered near paralysis upon seeing him enter the ring. That was the power of one, literally and figuratively. Iron Mike had it; he won all thirty-seven fights in his first five years of professional boxing, with thirty-three of those wins coming by way of knockouts in early rounds.

The power of one served him well for awhile, but when he began to have problems outside the ring, problems with the law and with people, Mike Tyson had no extra power to help him. He lacked a higher power in his life to put him back on track. He started with the power of one, and that was all that he had. His life story demonstrates clearly the inadequacy of the power of one.

Some will say that with a bit more discipline and self control, Tyson's decline and fall would not have been as sharp and debilitating as it was. Perhaps so, perhaps not. The lesson to be drawn is that Tyson relied exclusively on the power of one. It served him well and took him as far as it could have taken him. The power of one is limited in its scope and application. One can rely on that power only to a limited extent. It is only a matter of time before its inadequacy is exposed.

Mike Tyson is a person who relied completely on the power of one: his own abilities, his own strength, his own efforts and determination.

It initially worked very well for him, but its limitations soon began to show. When personal problems led to difficulty in his marriage and in his dealings with people in general, he became distracted from his boxing career. He had no extra power to bring him back in line. Tyson had no higher power to work with him. There was no partnership with a divine being in his life. It was just his power, sheer power, and that was not enough to keep him at such lofty heights.[1]

He did rise to greatness and superstar status. In fact, for the second half of the 1980s Mike Tyson was a megastar. But not long after that, it all began to fall away. His story is like a shooting star which dazzled the skies for a brief period and then was gone.

In 1988 Mike Tyson demolished the previously undefeated Michael Spinks. Tyson did the job in only ninety-one seconds and earned a whopping twenty million dollars. Over the period of his career Tyson reportedly earned more than four hundred million dollars. Yet in 2003 he filed for bankruptcy, having struggled financially for some time. He was broke, and he was broken. He was broken financially; he was broken mentally; he was broken psychologically; he was broken emotionally. The boxer who achieved megastar status was now operating on the fringes. The mystique was gone.

In 2005 at only thirty-nine years of age Iron Mike was reported to have appraised his life thus: "I'm really a sad, pathetic case." He went on, "My whole life has been a waste. I've been a failure." He also said, "I just want to escape. I'm really embarrassed with myself and my life. I want to be a missionary."[2]

Tyson was destined for greatness. He did achieve it briefly but only with the power of one. He could not sustain it. Obviously, he could have done a lot better with some discipline and self control, but the point still remains that he was relying on his own power, his own abilities, his willpower, his strength, and his determination. They served him well for a time, but the power of one is ultimately inadequate. He did not have additional firepower in his arsenal. Tyson did not have a higher power to work in partnership with him. He did not have divine power to guide him and shield him, and thus, he was totally exposed. In the interview previously quoted Tyson also said, "I'll never be happy.

I believe I'll die alone . . . I'm really lost, but I'm trying to find myself."[3] With the power of two, he would never have felt that way, because he would have known himself and his mission.

The Soccer Genius

He was born in Villa Fiorito, a shantytown on the southern outskirts of Buenos Aires, to a poor family. He was discovered by a talent scout at age ten, and in 1976 he made his debut with Argentinos Juniors. He signed his first professional contract as a player at age fifteen. The following year, he became the youngest player ever to play with the Argentina national soccer team. He was to have an illustrious professional soccer career that stretched from 1977 to 1997. During those twenty years, he dominated the sport in Spain, Italy, and his home country of Argentina.

In 1982, he played in his first Soccer World Cup. In his second World Cup in 1986, he led his national team to victory against West Germany. He was widely regarded as the best player of that tournament, but he became a legend because of two goals he scored in the quarterfinal game against England. He scored the first goal by pushing the ball past the England goalkeeper with his hand. The referee thought he headed it and ruled it as a legitimate goal. It became widely known as the "Hand of God Goal," because the player later implied that God was ultimately responsible for that goal. Later in the same match, he displayed his genius when he ran half the length of the soccer field, beating five English players as well as their goalkeeper, to score his second goal. Argentina won that match. In 2002, his famous goal was voted "Goal of the Century" in an online poll conducted by FIFA.

His name is Diego Armando Maradona, the greatest soccer player of recent times. He also captained Argentina to the 1990 World Cup. His team got to the finals but lost to Germany. He retired from soccer in 1997. He won many awards at the club level, national level, and international level. Notable among them, in 2000 he was voted in an official FIFA poll as the Player of the Century.

What is the relevance of this story to the power of two? Diego Maradona rose to greatness in soccer. He was a megastar, and unlike

Iron Mike his reign was not exactly brief, because his career spanned some twenty years. He was the most famous and most highly paid soccer player of his time. Nevertheless, Maradona's life story demonstrates that he relied on the power of one. He was extraordinarily talented on the soccer field. He was short, but he had strong physique and low centre of gravity which gave him advantage over other players. The midfield player was a wizard with the ball, and he could dribble at full speed. He also had the mental and psychological attitude for soccer; he had vision and strategy. These talents served him very well and propelled him to greatness and megastar status in soccer.

However, he was operating on the power of one, and its limitations soon began to show. Maradona had no additional firepower. He had no higher power to work with hand in hand. Rather, he relied completely on his own power, and when he began to have serious problems, he allegedly turned to drugs for assistance. This proved to be his Achilles' heel. In fact, in his third World Cup in 1994, he was sent home in disgrace for failing a doping test. It was not the first time. He has allegedly had problems with drugs since the 1990s and spent some time in Cuban and Swiss detox clinics.

Maradona was one of the greatest soccer stars of the twentieth century. He is a legend, but his greatness is flawed. It is incomplete. With his extraordinary natural genius, he could have achieved much more, both on the field and off. He could have given much more to his community. But the power of one was insufficient to give him completeness and true greatness. He did not have another power, a higher power, to assist him.

Summary

The case studies discussed in this chapter demonstrate clearly how the power of two is meant to work and also how it should not work. The cases of Great Grandpa Adam and King Saul taught us many lessons. The first lesson is that those two people started very well in life. They started with the power of two. They worked with God in ultimate partnerships, and so they rose to greatness. Great Grandpa Adam was in charge of the Garden of Eden, and he used to walk and chat with God. Saul was a successful king of Israel for many years. But we learned from those cases that, once they violated their partnerships with God and began to operate with the power of one, their downfall was imminent. The cases show that with the power of two, they rose to greatness and continued to remain great. However, once they abandoned the ultimate partnerships with God and began to rely on their own powers, they failed. They lost their greatness and superstar status, and they just faded away.

The two contemporary case studies we examined showed clearly that with the power of one a person can achieve a lot in life. In fact, with the power of one a person can achieve greatness and even megastar status. But the inadequacy of the power of one soon begins to reveal itself, and if the person has no higher power to rely on, he will easily lose direction in life. He ends up in disastrous situations and does not know how to get out of them, because there is no extra firepower to call on.

With the power of one, you are on your own and when things start to go awry, there is no higher power to bring you back in line. You may rise to greatness with the power of one, but it will not last long. At the minimum, you will lack personal fulfillment.

Finally, in your own community, city, or country you know of people who were destined for greatness or superstar status and who have since faded away. These were people who showed great promise at an early age; some even showed great promise in more than one field. They excelled in sports, music, entertainment, drama, academics, or another area. They were shaping up to be leaders and champions in their fields. Much was expected of them from their communities. The sky was the limit for them and achieving greatness and fame was only a matter of time.

But where are they now? In some countries, the media runs newspaper articles or TV programs called "Where Are They Now?" trying to track the careers of those who showed early promise in certain fields. Often the individuals are hard to trace. They lost direction and faded away before they made it to stardom, or they were not able to sustain a high level of greatness. They disappeared into obscurity. Such people abound in the sports and music worlds, but you can also find them in all other areas. It could be a person next door to you or a former schoolmate. The most likely explanation for their fading away is that they were relying on the power of one, and it was patently inadequate. The power of two is the answer.

Power 2 Principles

The case studies examined in this chapter clearly show that the power of one is inadequate to lift a person to greatness or sustain their superstar status.

Many people who showed great promise earlier in their lives have fallen by the wayside, because they had no higher power to rely on.

With the power of two, you can rise to greatness and sustain it.

With the power of two, you will find fulfillment in your life.

CHAPTER THREE

A Partnership in Everyday Life

A person standing alone can be attacked and defeated,
but two can stand back-to-back and conquer . . .

—ECCLESIASTES 4:12

Then make me truly happy by agreeing
wholeheartedly with each other,
loving one another, and working together
with one heart and purpose.

—PHILIPPIANS 2:2

I am a lawyer by training, and I practiced law for many years in Australia. I know for a fact that numerous law firms operate as partnerships. But partnerships are not limited to law firms. On the contrary, partnerships can be found in most professions, such as engineers, doctors, dentists, accountants, financial advisors, real estate agents, and so on. In fact, partnerships are so common these days that they can be found all across the business spectrum, from small businesses to large corporations.

Furthermore, partnerships do not operate only in the private sector. They are also used in public organizations. For example, there can be a partnership between two governmental departments. There can also be a partnership between a federal government and a state government, or between a state government and a local government. In more recent times, there has emerged what is described as a public-private partnership.

Partnerships number in the hundreds of thousands in most countries–even in the millions in some developed countries. This is clear evidence of their popularity.

Definition

A partnership is a relationship between two or more persons who join together to carry on a business, trade, or other enterprise. The individuals work together to operate the business or trade by contributing money, assets, and skills. They share in the profits or losses of the enterprise. In a traditional partnership, the partners operate as individuals, so in the event of loss, they share the liability. The responsibility could extend to their personal assets, including their homes and personal possessions. Some countries now recognize a limited liability partnership. The limited liability partnership is required to be registered by law and has some features that protect it from personal liability. Throughout this book, we are concerned with the traditional, standard type of partnership, which is accepted in most countries of the world. We will restrict ourselves to that definition.

Features of a Partnership

All partnerships have certain common features. To start with, the partners are not employees of the partnership. Rather, the partners operate as individuals in their own right. As a consequence, in most countries the partnership itself does not pay a tax. Rather, the individual partners pay taxes to the government.

It is now standard practice to have the terms of a partnership put in writing, though it is possible to operate one on a less formal basis. It is critical for the partners to agree on the terms by which the partnership will operate before they open for business. Usually, the partnership agreement will cover the following matters:

- Names and Purpose. The persons forming the partnership will be listed, and the nature or purpose of the business will be clearly identified.
- Contributions. Contributions to the partnership are spelled out and the ownership percentage of each partner is recorded.
- Allocation of Profits, Losses, and Withdrawals. Allocation rules are clearly defined.
- Authority of the Partners. It is usual to have a senior partner, and so the authority of the senior partner vis-à-vis the other partners is explained. If this is not done, one partner may make decisions without receiving prior consent from the other partners, which could bind the entire partnership.
- Rules of Operation. This explains how the partners would like to operate their business or trade. It includes such matters as management, decision making, and rules of conduct.
- Term or Duration. For example, the partnership agrees to commence on a specified date and remain in operation until terminated, as provided for in the agreement.
- Resolving Conflicts. A specified format for how to deal with conflicts between partners.
- Termination. The circumstances under which the partnership will come to an end.

One of the distinct advantages of a partnership is its flexibility. It is not like a formal company that is restricted by rules and regulations on how it must operate. A partnership is quite flexible, and its operation is entirely up to the partners. As stated earlier, it is even possible to have a partnership agreement that is not in writing. But in today's world, it is the norm to ensure that people going into a partnership agree on the terms in writing.

Now that we have a common understanding of the definition of a partnership, we can move on to discuss the power of two, also known as the ultimate partnership.

Power 2 Principles

A distinguishing feature of a partnership is that it is inherently flexible.

There are no predetermined rules for a partnership. The partners can modify the terms at any time

PART TWO

the power
of two in
PRACTICE

CHAPTER FOUR

Establishing the Ultimate Partnership

The Unique Nature of This Partnership

Can two people walk together without
agreeing on the direction?

—Amos 3:3

As we have just established, a partnership in general is created between two or more individuals. It may be a small partnership, or it may be a large one. There may be a provision in the partnership agreement for the admission of more partners into the business as time goes by. In contrast, the unique feature of the ultimate partnership is that it exists only between two. There is no room in this partnership for others to be involved. It is the power of two, and no one else is involved in the partnership.

Throughout history, God has worked through individuals. God does not like to work through committees, boards of management, assemblies, or the like. God always chooses a single person through whom to work. Thus, when God wanted to liberate the Israelites from Egypt, he chose one person, Moses. When Moses died, God chose Joshua. When God wanted to plant an Israelite in the pharaoh's palace to make preparations to feed his people during the upcoming period of famine, he chose one person, Joseph. Similarly, God chose one person, Abraham, to be the father of many nations. He did not choose several people, but rather just one person. When God decided to send a savior to liberate his people on earth, he sent one person, Jesus. He did not send a heavenly host of angels. He sent one man. The list goes on and on.

God works in the same way today, and he enjoys anointing individuals. God wants to work with you and you alone in the ultimate partnership. The partnership is between you and your higher power. We have already emphasized the point that God created you for a purpose. He gave you unique qualifications for the mission he had in mind even before you were born. He tailor made you for that mission.

We have also emphasized the point that God wants to work with you to achieve the mission. He is passionate about working with you. Hence, the parties in this ultimate partnership are you and your God only. There is no one else involved. God may use you to assist another person in achieving his or her destiny. Similarly, God may use another person to assist you in achieving the mission he has set for you. But no third person is involved in the partnership. It is just you and your God.

We also stressed earlier that you should see the higher power in this ultimate partnership as your own. He is your own personal God. It is, therefore, necessary for you to have an intimate relationship with him. You should not see your partner as the God of a significant denomination or expansive religious community. This person you are entering into the ultimate partnership with is your God. It's personal. Sure, many others may have this same God as their own. There is nothing wrong with that. But for optimal operation of the power of two, the only thing that matters is that he is your God, your personal God, who has created you as an individual. He has made you a unique person, and you should deal with him as your very own.

The Fundamentals

Teach me to do your will, for you are my God.
May your gracious Spirit lead me forward
on a firm footing.

—PSALM 143:10

As we saw in the definition of partnerships, there are certain common features. In fact, there are some fundamentals which ought to be present in any partnership, though the actual details are up to the persons involved. The ultimate partnership follows the same basic pattern, and so the fundamentals are the same.

The Partners

We have just stated that in the ultimate partnership you and God are the only partners. Obviously, you must know your partner. You cannot enter into a partnership with somebody you don't know. In a standard partnership, you obtain as much background information as possible about a potential partner before entering into a business arrangement with him or her.

The same principle applies to the ultimate partnership. Therefore, if you do not already have a relationship with God, it is critical that you take steps to invite him into your life before proceeding further. If you already know God but do not have a personal relationship with him, again, you need to take immediate steps to invite him into your life for an intimate relationship. Additionally, if you have always regarded God as a mighty, awesome, authority figure, far away in the heavens, you must alter that view. To enter into and operate the ultimate partnership, you need to develop a very close relationship with your higher power. It will enable you to work hand in hand. If you are not sure how to go about this, you will find some recommendations at the end of this chapter to get you started.

Let me emphasize once again, you need to know God, your partner, in order to operate the power of two. It is a sine qua non—an essential part of the power of two. There is no other way.

God is your own personal God, so you may call him by whatever name you prefer. You need to state his name in the ultimate partnership. You may call him: My God, My Lord, My Savior, My Yahweh, My Jesus, My Christ, My El Shaddai, My Jehovah Rapha, My Jehovah Shammah, My Jehovah Jireh, My Redeemer, My Refuge, My Rock, My Fortress, My Father, My Deliverer, My Shepherd, or any other name you prefer. The choice is yours, but please don't just call him God. Add the pronoun "my" to the name. That is a first step in personalizing your relationship.

The Purpose

In a standard partnership, there is a clear purpose for which the business is set up. Someone starts with an idea, it becomes crystallized into a definite plan, and it brings people together to form a partnership. The partners aim to run the business or trade to achieve that purpose or plan.

Similarly, your ultimate partnership has a purpose. We have touched on it several times. God has a mission for you on earth. In Psalm 139:3, the Bible says that God has charted your path ahead of you. In Jeremiah 29:11, God assures you that the plans he has for you are plans for good and not for disaster; plans to give you a future and a hope. You have a destiny, and the ultimate partnership will help you achieve that goal.

You must know why you are on this earth. If you do not know, then your life is aimless. You could be living a life without direction or purpose. This is one major reason why many people do not find fulfillment and peace in life. They are here on earth, and they are having a good time, but they do not know why they were placed on earth in the first place. A person can be successful in his or her profession and yet find that life is meaningless. A person can have all the material comforts in the world and yet feel empty inside. A person can be a powerful and influential person in a country, in a business conglomerate, in a service organization, or in a community organization and yet feel that there is something seriously missing in his or her life. The explanation is that they do not know why they are on this earth. They are not aware of the mission for which God created them. They may seem to enjoy life, but in actual fact they are a mess inside.

Therefore, it is very important to know your mission in life, so that you do not lead a life which in the end will be wasted. Once you get into an ultimate partnership, you will learn your mission in life. Once you start working together with God, he will reveal your mission in life, as Psalm 138:8 explains.

This book will assist you in ascertaining your mission and getting on a path to your destiny. God does not want to have you in a partnership for the heck of it. On the contrary, God desires to go into partnership with you, so that the two of you can combine and achieve the mission for which he created you and placed you on this earth. Only God knows the nature of that mission. He has revealed missions to many people on earth, and he will reveal yours to you. Not only will he reveal it to you, but he is desirous—may I say desperate—to work with you to achieve your destiny and his mission for you.

Communication

You cannot have a partnership with somebody if you are not able to communicate with that person. How will you discuss matters concerning the operation of the partnership? It is necessary for there to be communication between you and your God in the ultimate partnership. That is the way in which he will let you know about your mission. It is through communication that you can discuss the project on earth with him. It is also through communication that he can guide you, protect you, and equip you for the mission he has for you.

In everyday life communication is taken for granted, because in most cases the partners are physically present in the same location. They see each other daily or regularly, and so communication is easy. Even if a partner is away somewhere, it is not difficult to communicate in this day and age. A partner can easily be reached by telephone, email, or fax communication. Cell phones and email have greatly enhanced communication in modern times.

But you cannot reach your God by phone, email, or fax. Even the most sophisticated communication equipment cannot assist you. However, as I have been stressing all along, you need to recognize and deal with your God on a personal level. You have to be in regular communication or communion with him. Please do not assume this will be difficult or impossible. I communicate with my God on a regular basis, and I am not alone. Millions of people around the world communicate with their God daily.

The difference here is that in the ultimate partnership you have to communicate with him more frequently and in a personal way. I communicate with my God on a daily basis through prayer and praise. In my praises I thank him for the things he has done for me during the day. I thank him for tiny, little things, and I also thank him for great, big things. I acknowledge and thank him publicly on Sundays through my worship at church. I glorify him, magnify his name, exalt him, and applaud him greatly. So I praise and worship my God both privately and publicly.

Showing your gratitude to God is an essential way to communicate with him. Through my prayers I tell my God about my concerns, issues, and problems. I ask him for help on a daily basis. I tell him about specific problems and issues and ask him for wisdom or direction to solve those problems. Sometimes, I ask him for a solution to the problem itself, but more often I ask him to lead me to the solution, to guide and prompt me into action.

If you do not communicate with God regularly, you may feel the need to introduce yourself all over again whenever you do decide to reach out to him. You may not be sure whether or not he recognizes you. That is a common perception with human beings, the idea that you must introduce yourself again to God if you have been absent from communication. He might not have forgotten you at all, but because you have not been communicating regularly, and now you need his help in a crisis, you will have a guilty feeling that he might not remember you or recognize your voice. So you reintroduce yourself to him.

I do not feel good about myself when I am in a situation where I have to introduce myself to somebody all over again. This is especially true when I desperately need help from that person, and I am not sure whether he or she remembers me. God will not have forgotten you, but you do not want to take that feeling to him when you are in dire straits over a matter.

As we all know, communication is not a one-way street. God also communicates with us in various ways. Some people say they cannot hear God. It means they have not been in regular contact with him. Once you are in regular contact with your own personal God, he will communicate with you just as regularly. God will communicate with you on small issues as well as the big issues. God does communicate with us in a variety of ways. They include dreams, visions, a gentle whisper, scripture, or a still, small voice. Sometimes God uses other human beings to communicate with us. God has many ways of communicating, but in the ultimate partnership you will learn the most preferred, most effective way by which God prefers to communicate with you. He may choose a different method for you than for me. He may also have another method for your spouse or child. Therefore, you should communicate with him on a daily or regular basis, and you will soon come to learn the preferred method he has chosen for you.

In my experience, my God prefers to communicate with me through the gentle whisper. My God has communicated with me countless times by this method. He has given me assurance when things looked bleak. He has given me specific answers to questions I have asked and much more. My wife's God rarely communicates to her by this method. He prefers to communicate to her through his word in the scriptures. Consequently, my wife has become adept at reading God's messages to her in the scriptures.

So, it is important to find out how God desires to communicate with you. Whichever method he chooses is entirely up to him. But for you, the options are severely limited. You send your requests to him by way of prayers—supplications, requests, or entreaties. You may decide to do this through a pastor or prayer warrior, or you may prefer to do it yourself. It is strongly recommended that you do it yourself, since you are a party to the ultimate partnership. As far as I am aware, prayer, praise, and worship are the only methods by which you and I can communicate with God. We send our concerns, issues, and problems to God in prayer, and we thank him through praise and worship. God has countless options of communicating with us. At the end of the day, what matters is that in order for the ultimate partnership to operate effectively and successfully, communication between you and your God is absolutely essential. Communication has to be regular and often.

Choice

In a standard partnership, the parties are free to decide whether to enter the partnership or not. In addition, once the partnership comes into operation, the partners are autonomous. They have a large range in which to operate, though they do so under the general umbrella of the partnership. There are rules to follow, and if those rules are not adhered to, there are consequences. By and large, the partners have a lot of say in how they operate within the business.

In the ultimate partnership, your God also gives you a large range in which to operate. For starters, you have a choice to enter into a relationship with him or not. Then you have a choice as to how far you want to go with God. To derive maximum benefit from the ultimate partnership, you should be willing to go all the way with your God. You should give the partnership your total commitment, dedication, and devotion.

That does not mean you become a slave and continually take instruction. Your God will give you choices on many occasions. He prefers that you work with him as a partner, and so he empowers you to make decisions voluntarily.

You are a partner, and so you are not expected to act like a robot or work within straightjacket rules. In the ultimate partnership, God expects you to make choices on many important matters. He wants you to choose to stick with him and work diligently with him, but he does not force you to do so.

Of course, there are consequences for whatever actions you take. If you make choices which result in a breach of the partnership, there will inevitably be consequences from your partner.

As C. S. Lewis so poignantly put it:

There are two kinds of people: those who say to God, "Thy will be done," and those to whom God says, "All right then, have it your way."

Operational Rules

In order for the ultimate partnership to work effectively and success-fully, there are operational rules which must be followed. These rules are not one-sided. They work both ways. You have some obligations to perform and so does your God. Fortunately, God has set out the obli-gations and expectations in writing. It is now up to you to accept them and then fulfill your side of the bargain. On his deathbed, King David told his son Solomon:

> Observe the requirements of the Lord your God and follow all his ways. Keep each of the laws, commands, regulations, and stipulations written in the law of Moses so that you will be successful in all you do and wherever you go.
>
> —1 KINGS 2:3

Today, the commands, regulations, and stipulations cover all of those contained in the Bible. Equally importantly, they include those which your partner, God, will be giving to you directly as you communicate with him. He will not alter any of those contained in the Bible, but he is likely to give you further directions as you go along. In the succeeding chapters, we will discuss these operational rules and how they drive the ultimate partnership. For now, we will briefly go over a few core ones.

It is fundamental in the ultimate partnership for you to have faith in your partner. You cannot be in a partnership with your God if you do not have trust and confidence in him. Without trust, the partner-ship will not last long, if it starts at all. You must have faith in your God. You must be certain that he will perform his side of the bargain. You may not see things happening for quite some time. You may not see any concrete, visible evidence of the things God is doing for you or on your behalf. But if you have faith in him, you will rest assured that he is working behind the scenes, and it is only a matter of time before events will start to be revealed.

When you have faith in your God, you can have an effective part-nership with him. He will be there for you, and you will be there for him, too. You will be working together. The Bible tells us that without faith, it is impossible to please God (Hebrews 11:6). So no matter what you are capable of doing or whatever skills or resources you bring to the partnership, you will fall short if you do not have faith. God is most interested in your faith in him, your belief that he will deliver on his promises and always be there for you. It is faith; call it blind faith, which underpins the ultimate partnership. Your loud praises, vigorous worship, sacrifices, giving, and other good works are not sufficient in the eyes of God. It is your faith that will please him.

There is a story of a Christian who professed to believe in God. He once went mountain climbing, and suddenly a thick mist enveloped the whole area. As he groped around to find his way, he fell off a cliff. He managed to grab a tree branch on his way down to break his fall, and his heart began pumping with fear and trepidation. When he managed to recollect himself, he shouted, "Help! Help! Help! Is anyone out there?"

A voice boomed back, "Yes. God."

The gentleman then said, "Please help! Please help! Please help! Please help!"

God replied, "Let go off that tree branch!" The gentleman went silent, and so God said again, "I am God. I say let go off that tree branch!"

The man remained silent for some time, and then he shouted, "Is there anyone else out there?" He hung on to the tree branch for hours. When the mist cleared, he found that he was only a few feet from the ground.

It had been a true test of faith, and the supposed believer failed miserably. Proverbs 3:5 teaches us that we should trust the Lord with all our hearts and not depend on our own understanding. We should seek his will in everything, and he will direct us. The character in the story chose to rely on himself instead of the God he professed to believe in.

Another important operational rule is that you must obey the commands of your God. The ultimate partnership requires that you perform the duties which you have agreed to perform and desist in getting involved in activities that take you away from your relationship with God. Like faith, obedience is a cardinal element of the partnership. Failure to obey the terms of the agreement can lead to termination or other serious consequences.

As we saw earlier, the disobedience by Great Grandpa Adam and King Saul led to the termination of their partnerships with God. In the case of Great Grandpa Adam, he was banished from the Garden of Eden and certain curses were visited upon him and his wife. When King Saul first disobeyed God, his dynasty was denied the opportunity to reign over Israel forever. At that stage God did not disempower him. When he disobeyed a second time, God terminated the partnership and removed his power. King Saul was then possessed by a tormenting spirit. The Bible says, "Obedience is far better than sacrifice" (1 Samuel 15:22).

Like faith, your obedience will endear you to God. No amount of sacrifices, giving, or good works is more pleasing to God than obedience of his commands, his laws, or his dictates. For the ultimate partnership to work, your obedience must take priority over anything else that you can do for God.

God has made it clear that he will abide by the terms of an agreement, and he will not go back on his word (Psalm 89:34). His record is impeccable. We can be certain that once we enter into a partnership with God, he will honor all the obligations and undertakings of that partnership. In Numbers 23:19 it is stated that God will neither lie nor change his mind, because he is not a human being.

Another operational rule of the ultimate partnership is that God will never fail you, forsake you, or abandon you, as long as you are in partnership with him (Hebrews 13:5; Joshua 1:5). He will be there for you and with you through thick and thin. Wherever you go and whatever you do, you will have confidence that you are not alone. When the storms of life come, you know that you have a superior power by your side, and he will see you through them all.

Yet another important element of the ultimate partnership is that God will bless you and allow you to prosper as long as you are in partnership with him. After God made a covenant with Abraham, he blessed him and destined him to be the father of many nations (Genesis 17:4).

That promise alone was a great blessing to someone who was advanced in age and had little hope of ever having a child of his own. Abraham was almost a hundred years old, and his wife was ninety. But God did not rest there. He blessed Abraham in all aspects of his life. Abraham became a great man of wealth and prosperity (Genesis 24:1 & 34). Furthermore, God blessed Isaac and Jacob, the son and grandson of Abraham. God kept his promise to Abraham that he would bless him and use him to be a blessing to others.

In a similar way, when you enter into an ultimate partnership with your God, he will not only bless you with abundance, but he will also bless your children and grandchildren and use you to be a blessing to others.

The Ultimate Partnership Agreement

1. This Ultimate Partnership is made between, My God (or My Savior, My Lord, My Jesus, My Jehovah Jireh, My El Shaddai, etc.) and myself.
2. I agree to fully comply with and obey all the terms, promises, and obligations of this partnership.
3. I enter into this partnership of own my free will.
4. I understand that if I violate any of the terms of this partnership, there will be serious consequences for me including termination of the partnership.
5. My God also agrees to abide by the terms of this Ultimate Partnership in accordance with the promises, undertakings, and obligations set out in the Bible.

    My Name _____

    Signature _____

Made on this ____ day of _____ in the year _____ before and between God and myself.

Termination

By now, it is clear that there are certain circumstances which can bring the partnership to an end. One possibility is to end the partnership through mutual consent. The actions of a partner can also indicate that he or she no longer wishes to continue in the partnership. In that case, it is also clear that the partnership has come to an end. The cases of Great Grandpa Adam and King Saul are instructive in that regard.

Inviting God into Your Life

If you do not already have God in your life or you do not have a close relationship with him, inviting God into your life is an essential first step before you can enter into the ultimate partnership agreement. First you have to invite him into your life, and then you can start to develop a close relationship with him. What follows is my recommended prayer of invitation, but if you would like to craft your own, by all means do so. Do not wait another day. Take action today to invite God into your life to be your partner.

> Dear God, I pray that you come into my life this day.
> I accept you as my Lord and Savior, and I desire to
> have a close relationship with you from now on.
> Please forgive me all my sins, accept me, and come into my life.
> Dear God, fill me with your Holy Spirit
> and show me my mission in this life.
> In the name of your Son, Jesus Christ, I pray.
> Amen.

If you pray this prayer, you will soon see its effect on your life. It will bring you peace, a kind of peace which you cannot understand. It is the peace of God.

Next, you will need assistance in developing a relationship with God. My suggestion is that you equip yourself with materials that will coach you. You can get spiritual tapes, CDs, videos, and other publications from your local bookstore. You can also receive assistance by watching spiritual TV programs like God Channel, Word, Daystar, TCT, and many others. One of the best approaches is to join a fellowship with somebody who already has a relationship with God. A fellowship group or church will be immensely helpful. Seek help, and you will find it.

Please do not confuse the above actions with the ultimate partnership. The latter is between you and your God only. It is a deliberate agreement. But before you can reach that level, you need to develop a relationship with God. Then you will be in a position to call him your own God. It is an essential step toward the ultimate partnership.

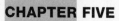

CHAPTER FIVE

Your God Will Empower You

*But when the Holy Spirit has come upon you,
you will receive power and will tell
people about me everywhere.*

—ACTS 1:8

Perhaps the most significant benefit that you will derive from the ultimate partnership is that your senior partner, God, will empower you. God will give you the extra firepower that you cannot otherwise obtain. With the power of one, you rely on your own power. We have seen that it is inadequate to propel you to greatness or sustain you once you have arrived. But once you enter into the ultimate partnership, God will grant you more potent power. God will add his supernatural, divine power to your own. This combination will bring into operation the power of two.

There are many examples, both in ancient and contemporary times, of God empowering those he chose for missions and special assignments.

Some Examples from History

We have already seen that when God chose Saul to be king of Israel, the first thing he asked his earthly representative, Samuel, to do was to anoint Saul. As soon as Saul was anointed, the spirit of God filled him. It came upon him "with power" (1 Samuel 10:6). God also changed his heart. Thus, Saul was transformed from an ordinary shepherd boy to a person fit to be a king. The prophet Samuel specifically told Saul that after the anointing, God would be with him. That is how the ultimate partnership works. Once you enter into it, God will empower you. It is the power of two which will propel you to superstar status. It is also that power that will sustain you once you have achieved greatness. After the anointing Saul was formally acclaimed king of Israel.

Again, when God found "a man after his own heart," the first thing he did was to empower him. God sent the same Samuel to anoint David to be king of Israel, after he became disappointed with Saul and terminated the partnership with him. When Samuel anointed David, "the Spirit of the Lord came mightily upon him from that day on" (1 Samuel 16:13).

We know from the Bible that David was already a very tough boy. He fought lions and bears, and he was not a person lacking courage or bravery. But despite those impressive credentials, it was still the power of one. David knew God, but at that point he only had the power of one. It was the anointing that made the difference. The anointing took David to a higher level. He no longer had to rely on his brute strength. He now had additional power that he could marshal.

I am sure you know the story of David and Goliath very well (1 Samuel 17:32–48). Everybody knows it, and we all love it. We love the fact that a young man is able to stand up to a bully. We love the fact that David came to the rescue of Israel when they were being intimidated and harassed by Goliath. Nobody likes to see bullies get away with their form of intimidation. But what they do not often tell you about the David and Goliath story is that at the time the confrontation took place, David had already been anointed. So David did not face Goliath with his own power alone. David was already empowered by God to be a leader of the Israelites. David had extra ammunition, and the power of two was in full operation. It was the ultimate partnership that defeated Goliath.

Even Jesus, before he could start his ministry, had to be empowered by God. When John the Baptist baptized Jesus in the River Jordan, the spirit of God descended upon him (Matthew 3:16–17; Mark 1:9–11).

Jesus was empowered and ready to embark on the mission God put him on earth to fulfill.

It is revealing that immediately after the empowerment of Jesus, Satan sought to test him. Satan wanted to find out if he truly had the power of God in him, so Satan tempted him three times in the wilderness. Jesus was able to soundly defeat Satan on all three occasions. Jesus was by then operating the ultimate partnership with his father in heaven. He had the power of the Father and the Son combined in him. That power enabled him to thwart and defeat Satan, not only on that occasion, but throughout his ministry.

Some Contemporary Examples

In contemporary times we can also cite numerous people who have been empowered by God to carry out their missions on earth. The list is too long to attempt to produce here. The mere idea of putting together such a list is mind-boggling. It is just not possible. I will discuss only two people here, but I am sure that you know many other examples. Certainly, you have read or heard of people in recent history who rose to prominence because they had the anointing of God.

The first person I want to mention here is Billy Graham. Today Billy Graham is an evangelist megastar. He is perhaps the greatest evangelist of our time. Known as the "pastor to presidents" because a number of U. S. presidents have consulted him, Billy Graham has had a huge impact around the globe. Born in the final days of World War I in Charlotte, North Carolina, William F. Graham made a personal commitment to Jesus Christ at age sixteen. He first gained international prominence in 1949 with a crusade he organized in Los Angeles. From there on, it was a steady rise to superstar status.

Billy Graham grew up on his father's dairy farm in North Carolina. Once he made his commitment to Christ, God empowered him mightily. Billy Graham then rose to become the greatest evangelist of our time. Today he still remains a megastar. His accolades, awards, and achievements are too many to document here, but it should be stated that he has preached the gospel to more people in live audiences than any other preacher in recorded history. He has personally preached to more than 210 million people in more than 185 countries. If we were to include those he has reached through TV, radio, and other media, the numbers would be in billions. Billy Graham has preached, not only in the United States, but also in Europe, Africa, Australia, the Middle East, and across the world. At the height of the Cold War, he was the first Christian to discuss the gospel with communist leaders in places like Budapest, Moscow, Pyongyang, and Beijing.

Billy Graham is unquestionably the greatest evangelist of this era and one of the greatest of all time. Billy Graham started on his father's farm, like Saul. But once he entered into an ultimate partnership with God, he never looked back or wavered in his commitment. As he once put it, his single purpose in life has been to help people develop a personal relationship with God. It has been a personal crusade for him. Billy Graham was empowered when he committed himself to God, and that ultimate partnership propelled him to greatness. Now in his eighties, Billy Graham is a living illustration of the power of two.

Let us look at another contemporary example. He was born on June 9, 1957, in South Charleston, Western Virginia. He started from humble beginnings, and he founded a tiny church called the Greater Emmanuel Temple of Faith in 1979. Today he is widely regarded as one of the greatest preachers in the world. His church, The Potter's House, is described as one of the fastest growing mega-churches in America. It has more than 30,000 members with fifty-nine active outreach ministries.

We are talking about Bishop T. D. Jakes. His preaching has been described as virtuosic. He is rigorous in his theology and is often quoted by preachers of note. Starting with a church of only 10 members, T. D. Jakes rose to megastar status once he made a commitment to God. Today, he is widely regarded as one of the greatest preachers of our time. He has been compared to Billy Graham and has also consulted with presidents of the United States. His counsel has been sought by leaders of other countries, as well, including Ghana, Nigeria, and Trinidad. He was a guest of the king of Jordan, King Abdullah II.

Bishop Jakes's sermons are broadcast to millions of people daily around the world. He is particularly noted for his courage in tackling issues in America such as abuse, which is considered a taboo topic by some churches. He has a special interest in prison ministry, and his TV preaching is broadcast to hundreds of prisons in the United States. God has truly empowered him since he entered into partnership with him.

It is the aim of Bishop T. D. Jakes to let his congregation and others experience God in all aspects of their lives. Therefore, he does not focus only on his church sermons and pastoral activities. Often referred to as the "Shepherd to the Shattered," T. D. Jakes is equally famous for his entrepreneurial vision, his philanthropy, and his humanitarian work. His Potter's House runs many programs for the poor and the downtrodden.

In 2005, when President George Bush was severely criticized for his handling of the Hurricane Katrina catastrophe in New Orleans, it was widely reported that Bishop T. D. Jakes was one of those to whom President Bush turned for help. The Bishop was also the keynote speaker at Bush's National Day of Prayer in September 2005.

Bishop T. D. Jakes rose from humble beginnings to greatness. When he started his ministry, he could not afford a car. At one point, the electricity and water to his house were cut off, because he could not pay the bills. Today he is a megastar, but he is where he is because God put him there. Once he entered into an ultimate partnership with God, he began to soar. He is still soaring, because he remains in partnership with God and has his empowerment. The power of two is operating in T. D. Jakes's life to keep him working together with God to achieve God's purpose on earth.

Summary

When you enter into the ultimate partnership with your God, he will empower you. It is one of the most significant benefits of entering into such a relationship. If the senior partner cannot bring additional power into the relationship, then what is the point of going into that relationship? That is the big difference between the ultimate partnership and an ordinary relationship. When you enter into the former, your God will anoint you. He will empower you, and this empowerment will last as long as you remain in the partnership with him. It is this extra power which combines with yours to generate the power of two. With the power of two you will be ready to rise to greatness.

Let me emphasize here that I have used the examples of Billy Graham and T. D. Jakes because they are outstanding individuals, and they are easily recognizable as having the power of God within them. I hope I have not given you the impression that God empowers only famous preachers. There are countless people whom God has anointed to fulfill various missions on earth, and most of these people are not pastors or priests. I want to point out that God empowers all those who enter into partnership with him from all walks of life.

The ultimate partnership is not confined to the ministry. On the contrary, it applies to all areas of life on earth, because God needs people to work everywhere. He empowers people in sports, music, the entertainment industry, the military, service organizations, and businesses, to name a few areas. There is no place in which God does not operate, and so he anoints and is ready to empower people in every imaginable spot.

If you look around you, you will find evidence of this in your own town or country. Next time they have an awards night for entertainers or athletes, pay particular attention to the number of award winners who say they attained their achievements through the power of God. They may not use the term ultimate partnership, but in essence they will be telling you about exactly that.

Power 2 Principles

When you enter into the ultimate partnership with your God, he will anoint you. He will fill you with some of his own power. You will then have the power of two.

Throughout history, God empowered people on earth.

Today, God is still empowering people in all walks of life.

CHAPTER SIX

Your God Will Provide You with the Resources

And God will generously provide all you need.
Then you will always have everything you need
and plenty left over to share with others.

—2 Corinthians 9:8

Just as your God will empower you when you enter into the ultimate partnership with him, he will also provide you with the resources you need to accomplish the mission he has set for you. How can your God, your personal God, give you an assignment and seriously expect you to struggle on your own? What would be the meaning of the partnership if you still had to struggle to find the necessary resources to achieve the mission which God planned for you long before you were born?

Your God does not want you to rely on your power of one, but rather he wants you to operate with the power of two. He will gladly provide you with the resources you need to fulfill your mission. God has given this assurance in Philippians 4:19. In fact, when you consider it on a deeper level, providing you with resources is part of empowering you. Giving you the power to operate includes the resources to operate. In fact, empowerment from God is comprised of the actual spiritual power and the power to obtain or use resources.

Again, we will use historical and contemporary examples to illustrate the points in this chapter.

Some Examples from History

In the Bible

One important example from history is Joseph. We are not told exactly when Joseph made his partnership with God, but we do know that God was with Joseph throughout his life. God was with him from his childhood days, when he started to have spiritual dreams, until his death.

The important point here is when God chose Joseph to be the person to feed Jacob's family and the Israelites as a whole during the period of famine. God made sure he got Joseph into Pharaoh's palace well in advance. It was a long-term strategic move on the part of God, which neither Joseph, his father, his brothers, nor anyone else could have understood. By putting Joseph into Pharaoh's palace, God placed all the resources of Egypt at Joseph's disposal. God gave Joseph the resources to carry out the mission he planned for him long before he was born, the mission he hinted at in dreams when Joseph was a little boy (Genesis 37–50). It should be mentioned that once Joseph entered Pharaoh's palace, he remained there until his death. In other words, Joseph enjoyed greatness and prosperity until his death.

A second example is that of Moses. When God first called him on the edge of the desert, Moses gave several excuses for why he could not go back to Egypt and liberate God's people. God empowered him for the mission anyway. God said that he would be with him always (Exodus 3:12). But Moses still made excuses that he was not fit for the assignment.

God then asked Moses what he had in his hand. Moses replied that it was a simple shepherd's staff, a rod. God provided him with the resources for the mission by empowering the shepherd's staff (Exodus 4:2–5). From then on, it was not an ordinary staff. It became part of Moses, very much like a companion. More importantly, God turned an ordinary rod into a formidable weapon against Pharaoh and the Egyptians. Thus, the shepherd's staff transformed from a simple piece of wood to an important resource Moses would use, not only against Pharaoh, but also to split the Red Sea, to obtain water from a rock, and to accomplish many other supernatural tasks. Through the rod,

Moses was able to secure many victories in the name of God and for the Israelites as a whole.

But the shepherd's staff was not the only resource God provided Moses. God also taught him how to perform miracles which would convince the Israelites and Pharaoh's court that he had God's power within him (Exodus 4:6–8).

Furthermore, God got Moses's brother, Aaron, to work with him, specifically to be his spokesman (Exodus 4:10–14). We see here God's empowerment of Aaron as well. As the Bible records it, Aaron was at Moses's side from when God called him until Aaron's death. Aaron and Moses never parted company, just as Moses always kept his staff close to his side.

We can see clearly in this case that God fully provided Moses with the resources he needed for the mission God gave him, which was to liberate the Israelites from Egypt. Once God empowered Moses and granted him the necessary resources, he no longer had any excuses not to go and carry out the assignment given to him.

The Bible records that God also brought additional resource to Moses in the form of people. Jethro, his father-in-law, provided valuable management advice (Exodus 18:13–27). Joshua and others were also brought in to assist Moses in his advanced years.

There are countless other examples in history of God providing the necessary resources to people for specific missions. When Saul was anointed king, God chose a group of advisers for him in his hometown of Gibeah (1 Samuel 10:26). When David was anointed king of Israel, God ensured that he first spent time in King Saul's palace to learn how a king's court operates (1 Samuel 16:14–23). It was essential training for the man who was to be the next king of Israel. Finally, it is well known that Jesus had twelve human resources working with him throughout his ministry.

Outside the Bible

Charles Haddon Spurgeon was born in Kelvedon, Essex, in the United Kingdom on June 19, 1834. At the age of fifteen, God called him to preach the gospel. He converted to Christianity, and God empowered and equipped him mightily. C. H. Spurgeon responded to the call of God and started preaching the gospel. He never went to a theological college, but Spurgeon was so empowered and equipped by God that he rose to greatness as a preacher within a short time.

At age twenty, he was made pastor of London's famous New Park Street Chapel. From then on he soared. Spurgeon pastored a church of almost 6,000 in London, a huge number in those days. C. H. Spurgeon's sermons became so popular that they were published in printed form every week and widely circulated—even as far as Australia. By the time of his death in 1892, Spurgeon had preached almost 3,600 sermons and published forty-nine volumes of commentaries, sayings, anecdotes, illustrations, and devotionals.

There is no doubt that C. H. Spurgeon rose to megastar status. He founded Sunday schools, churches (including what is today regarded as the first mega-church), an orphanage, the Pastor's College, and several mission stations. When God called him, he was only fifteen years old. He did not have a degree in theology, but God gave him the resources for his mission. Spurgeon operated an ultimate partnership with God. He is generally regarded as the greatest preacher of the nineteenth century and one of the greatest of all time. Today, his printed sermons are still very much in demand.

Similarly, D. L. Moody (1837–1899) came from a very poor background and had very little education when God called him. He was to the United States what C. H. Spurgeon was to the United Kingdom. At age seventeen he could barely read and write. At Bible College he searched for the Gospel of John in the Old Testament.

Coming from a poor background, D. L. Moody was only intent on making money and making it fast, but God had other ideas for him. Once D. L. Moody entered into an ultimate partnership with God, he took America by storm. God empowered him so tremendously that he rose to become one of the greatest preachers in America during that era. He became a prolific author, launched a Christian publishing house, and built schools, churches, and a Bible institute among other achievements.

Contemporary Examples

Ray McCauley was enthusiastically engaged in bodybuilding when he was called by God. He was reportedly once a runner-up to Arnold Schwarzenegger in the Mr. Universe Contest. He now pastors a church of more than 36,000 in Randburg, Johannesburg in South Africa. He started that successful church in his parents' living room in 1979.

When God called Ray McCauley, he empowered him and equipped him with the necessary resources for his mission. He went from winning bodybuilding contests to winning bodies and souls for God. Pastor Ray McCauley also played an important role in bringing apartheid to an end. Today he is one of the most influential people in South Africa and was once visited by President Nelson Mandela. Ray McCauley's preaching is broadcast to many countries in Africa and beyond. He is touching hundreds of thousands of lives through his Rhema Ministries. They are actively involved in programs for homeless children, HIV/AIDS hospices, orphanages, and programs to feed the hungry.

Ray McCauley is rising to superstar status because God transformed him from a bodybuilder to a winner of souls for the Lord. God has equipped him for his mission on earth. Ray McCauley is on his way to achieving his destiny.

Let's look at another example. She is unquestionably one of the leading evangelists of our time. She is certainly the best-known female evangelists in the world. She is the author of more than seventy books, many of them bestsellers. She preaches at conferences in many countries, and her sermons and teachings are broadcast to billions of people around the globe. She is none other than Joyce Meyer.

Her life did not start out successful. On the contrary, she had it very rough before the Lord called her. She was the victim of horrendous abuse: sexual abuse, verbal abuse, and emotional abuse. She had a limited education, and her life seemed to be one of hopelessness and helplessness. She was going nowhere.

But then God called her to preach the gospel to the ends of the earth, and she became empowered. God gave her all the resources she would need for her mission. She has been teaching the word of God since 1976, and she has been in ministry fulltime since 1980. It has not always been smooth sailing for Joyce Meyer, but God has been faithful to her. Today, she is full of God's anointing and she is touching lives around the world. She is in an ultimate partnership with God, and she has risen to greatness. She is doing wonderful things for God, and her power is still rising. Her daily TV program, *Enjoying Everyday Life*, which she hosts herself, is very popular around the globe, because it is practical and easy to understand. Joyce Meyer has also been recognized with high honors, such as being awarded honorary doctorates by leading universities in the United States.

Yet another instructive example is Matthew Ashimolowo. He was born on March 17, 1952, in Nigeria and raised as a Muslim. But God called him to preach the Christian gospel, and today Ashimolowo is the senior pastor of Kingsway International Christian Centre in London. His church is often described as the fastest growing church in Europe. Church services are held in shifts in a five thousand seat auditorium.

Matthew Ashimolowo also ministers in France, the Netherlands, Ghana, Nigeria, the United States, Canada, and other countries. He is the author of many books, and his sermons are broadcast on radio and TV to millions of people across Europe, Africa, Asia, Australia, and beyond. Matthew Ashimolowo is a rising star on the international stage. He is working in an ultimate partnership with God. Once the young Muslim was called to preach the gospel, God gave him the power and the resources to fulfill his mission.

Summary

When you enter into an ultimate partnership with God, he will not only empower you, he will also grant you the resources you need to carry out the mission he has for you. We have seen throughout history that God has been consistently equipping the persons he chooses for various missions. The contemporary examples teach us that God is still operating the same way today, and he will also equip you appropriately for whatever mission he has for you.

Providing you with the proper resources may take various forms. It will depend on your circumstances and the mission for which you have been called. We learned that in the case of Joseph, God positioned him in Pharaoh's palace well ahead of the famine which was to plague that region. In Pharaoh's palace, Joseph had at his disposal all of the resources of Pharaoh. That is how he was able to save God's people. Similarly, David was positioned into King Saul's court to enable him learn how to operate as a ruler. Sometimes, the resources a person needs to fulfill a mission may already be at hand. God asked Moses what he had in his hand. He replied that it was a shepherd's staff. Once God empowered it, it became a formidable weapon.

I have come across commentaries and sermons that say everything you need for your mission is in your own hands, and it is just a matter of making use of your gifts. However, this is a mistaken view. Having the shepherd's staff in his hand was not enough for Moses to do the powerful things he did. The difference is that God empowered what was in Moses's hand. It was the empowerment of God that turned it from an ordinary piece of wood into a formidable weapon of warfare against the mighty Pharaoh and his army.

The same applies to us today. We may already have what it takes to fulfill our destinies. It may be a gift or talent or an educational skill that we have obtained. The resources may be in the form of people already in our lives or who will be coming into our lives soon. It may even be that by virtue of inheritance or unique placement by God we already have access to substantial resources. All these elements may not be enough. What is really crucial is the empowerment God places on those resources. Once God puts his power into something, it transforms into an anointed weapon for the achievement of a divine purpose in our lives.

To this end, we should constantly bear in mind that the gifts and talents God has given us are not meant for our use only. They are meant for the benefit of many others, as well. Therefore, the talents or gifts you have are not meant to remain underutilized. That would frustrate God's broader purpose. Your gifts and talents are meant to touch many lives, so you should not keep them close to your chest. If you do so, you are failing in your duty to God and humanity. In Matthew 5:15, Jesus said that you should not hide your light. Instead, let it shine for all to see.

Let me emphasize once again that I used examples from Christian ministries because they could be easily verified and the information is well known. However, God's anointing and providing of resources is not confined to pastors or people who work in churches. It is available to all. It is available to you and me. God will do the same for you and me as he has done for those mentioned in this book.

Moreover, as I said before, it is impossible to list all the people who have been granted God's power and the resources to operate. There are thousands, perhaps millions who have been given the power of God and the resources to achieve their missions on earth. You may find such people in all walks of life. They are in sports, music, entertainment, the military, service organizations, businesses, and so on. They are everywhere, because God operates in all aspects of life. There is no area which is excluded by God. The examples I have used in this chapter only to serve as illustrations. As you can see, they are powerful illustrations of how you will be propelled to greatness if you enter into an ultimate partnership with God.

Power 2 Principles

When you enter into an ultimate partnership with your God, he will provide you with the resources you need to fulfill your mission on earth.

God will not let you struggle on your own. He will provide you with whatever you need.

The resource may be something you already possess, such as a gift or talent. It may also come in the form of a person in your life.

God must first anoint the resource to transform it into something that will help you achieve your mission in life.

CHAPTER SEVEN

You Need a Vision

But these things I plan won't happen right away.
Slowly, steadily, surely, the time approaches
when the vision will be fulfilled.

—HABAKKUK 2:3

I have a dream.

—DR. MARTIN LUTHER KING, JR.

In a business partnership, the partners need a vision to guide them to their goals. People don't just set up a partnership, open an office, and then sit and wait for customers to come through the door. Nor do people set up a partnership and then spend all their time counting their share of the profits. Business may not come in the door at all; profits may not be seen for a long time. The partners must have a plan to win business, retain customers, and make their partnership profitable.

In the business world, competition is cutthroat. No serious businessperson starts a business without a vision or a plan. People go into business for various reasons, and unfortunately some of those reasons are flimsy. I remember a former colleague of mine who left his job to start a law firm, because he was passed over for a promotion. He had not planned to start his own practice, but he was so angry at his employer that he quit. He did not make a solid plan when he left the firm and struck out on his own. He set up his own law practice merely because of the anger and frustration. The result was disastrous.

I know of other cases where people did not make a plan before going out into the business world. Some people went into business just to impress others, to boast that they were not wage slaves working for other people. The results were unfortunate, and I do not recommend it to anyone.

Research has shown that most small businesses fail in the first few years of operation—including partnerships. If you look around your own neighborhood, you will see the evidence. New shops or offices open for business with a lot of enthusiasm and fanfare. Before long, they quietly close their doors, and the owners disappear. Some years later, others come and use the same premises for a new business, and then history may repeat itself. It seems to be a universal phenomenon. It is not restricted to certain countries or cultures. It is the same in the United States, United Kingdom, Europe, Asia, Australia, and everywhere else in the world.

In some countries, the failure rate for new businesses is as high as 70 percent in the first year. In other countries it may be even higher. As the years accumulate, the failure rate drops. In many cases, if a small business can survive the first five years, the probability is quite high that it will make it. It is tough out there in the business world, and one cannot start a business without a vision. Do you remember the old adage that people don't plan to fail—they fail to plan? These days, we commonly talk of business plans, strategic plans, and the like. A partnership needs a vision to guide it to sustainability, growth, and profitability.

The Vision and Your Mission

Vision without action is a daydream.
Action without vision is a nightmare.

—JAPANESE PROVERB

In an ultimate partnership you also need a vision to guide you to your destination. Without a vision, how can you fulfill your destiny?

Without a vision, you will simply be wandering. You will be living from day to day, taking things as they come, but not exactly knowing where you are heading. Without a vision, you cannot get to where God wants you to be.

Your vision is the overall thing that you are aiming to attain. It is the big picture, the thing which you will be working toward well into the future. Your vision is just another term for your dream. You should dream big. However, your vision is not merely something that you vaguely desire, something that you hope will happen to you one day. Rather, your vision is a deliberate, intentional idea. You do not want to live your entire life and then at the end of it all not know why you were on earth. What a tragedy that would be! Sadly, a great number of people in this world are in precisely that situation. They do not know why they are on this earth.

Your vision will point you in a particular direction. Your vision will guide you and at the same time confine you to a path. With a vision, you will not be all over the place, swinging from one notion to the next, from one idea to another, with no real purpose. Your vision will keep you on target. It will give you focus.

The question you may be asking now is why you need to develop a vision when it is God who decides your mission on earth. Yes, it is God who decides your mission is on earth. He made that decision long before you were born. In fact, it is precisely for that reason that you were born, to fulfill your mission or destiny.

So the first thing you need to find out is what your mission on this earth is. You must ask your God that question when you enter into the ultimate partnership with him. You will remember that we discussed that one of the essential elements of the ultimate partnership is regular, preferably daily, communication with your personal God. When that communication is in operation, you should have no difficulty asking him anything. Believe me, he will communicate with you very clearly. It will be so clear that you will have no doubt in your mind about the message. Moreover, you can ask him for confirmation on the nature of your mission if you have any doubts. God has told many people what their missions are, and he will tell you also. When you learn your mission, write it down boldly. Stick it in a prominent place in your house, your office, or some other location where you will see it often.

You may be wondering if I know my own mission. I definitely know what my mission is in life today. I did not know it for more than forty years. Do you know why? Because for more than forty years I did not want to know God. To be more exact, I rejected God. I believed in myself and the philosophy of "I can do it; I will do it my way." My view was that I did not need God. That was how I conducted my life. I trained as a lawyer and practiced law for many years in Australia. My aim in life at that time was to be a very successful lawyer, a senior counsel, and perhaps a judge. I wanted to have all the comforts of life, such as a big house and a nice car, for my family and myself. I believed in myself and was confident in life.

I enjoyed law practice but I did not get as high as I had wanted. Later, I switched to university teaching. I rose to a senior level, and I was not doing badly in my work or in life. But I always felt that I was missing something. I did not want to have anything to do with God, and I laughed at those who believed in God. I used to say to them that their faith was a big joke. God had nothing to do with success and happiness in life. It all came from one's effort and determination. It was the power of one, and I relied heavily on it.

But recently, when I found God, I began to realize that there was more to life than achieving one's personal ambitions and acquiring material things. Throughout my life, I have always had the gift of writing, writing prolifically and in a way in which most people understand. When I was practicing law, I used to publish articles in law journals. When I was a professor, I was able to write even more successfully. I have about fifty publications to my name, including several books. My works are still being used in universities, particularly in Australia and the Asia Pacific region. In other words, I was not doing badly as an academic. Nevertheless, I did not have fulfillment.

Once I found God, I began to search for my mission in life. I began to ask myself what exactly God put me on this earth to do. I did not have to search very long. Actually, it was my wife who first drew my attention to my mission. God gave me the gift of writing from an early age. My wife impressed upon me that once God gives you a gift, he expects you to use it for his purposes and to bring him glory. Bingo! There it was. I asked God for confirmation and direction. That is why you are reading this book today. God has revealed to me that he wants me to use my gift of writing to teach people about him, to bring people to know him, and to bring him glory. I am convinced that this is my mission in life.

I spent most of my adult life practicing, teaching, or researching law, because that was my profession. I did not know God, and in fact I rejected him. Throughout all those years God had his eye on me and my mission. I developed and further enhanced my gift of writing. Today I am using it to fulfill my destiny.

The mission God has for you may be related to a gift or talent he gave you from the time you were born. Everyone has some gift. It is not difficult to find out what it is. It is usually something you are passionate about or something which comes naturally to you. It is the thing that stays with you, even when you change jobs, change careers, or change where you live. For me, my writing ability showed up as soon as I could read and write. Like most people, I had no particular encouragement to use it. I grew up as a normal kid and went to school in Africa, where the burdens of life did not allow most parents to nurture talents in their children at an early age. I grew up in a normal environment, but I could write at an early age. I tried my hand at poems and short stories when I was in primary school, but I had no one to help me with them. My writing ability showed up more clearly in college. I wrote some articles for national newspapers during those years. When I went into law practice, it did not extinguish my gift.

The point I am making is that you have a unique gift or talent, and it is God's will to use it. Your mission on earth will be related to that talent. But as we saw in the previous chapter, having a gift or talent is not enough. You need your God to anoint it and empower you through it. It is then that you can use it to fulfill your destiny. The empowerment of God is so essential that you cannot succeed without it. It is one of the benefits of entering into an ultimate partnership with your own God.

Having said all that, a person's mission in life is not always apparent. For some it is easy to see; for others it is not so easy. For example, when God called Moses, he made the mission clear to him. When God called Gideon, he also made the mission clear to him. But what about Joseph? Nobody knew what his mission was until he was in Pharaoh's palace and famine was imminent. God led Joseph through various challenges that finally brought him to Pharaoh's palace and his destiny.

We have seen in the contemporary examples that God calls people and makes their mission in life known to them. We discussed in the last chapter how God made it clear to C. H. Spurgeon, D. L. Moody, Ray McCauley, Joyce Meyer and Matthew Ashimolowo what exactly he wanted them to do. They responded to those calls, and they rose to greatness. In the same way, once you enter into an ultimate partnership with God, he will make your mission clear to you. If you already have a fair idea, seek confirmation from your personal God, and he will gladly tell you.

So in the ultimate partnership you need a clear strategy—a long-term strategy to achieve what God has set out for you to do. You cannot go aimlessly from day to day, idea to idea, and hope that it will all come to together in the end. It won't. You need to take specific action. You need to have a vision.

I am aware that some people tend to use the word *vision* to mean a distant future goal, final aim, or big picture. Then they use the word *mission* more precisely for immediate goals. They believe the vision should be the grand design, and the mission should be the more clearly defined approach. I am also aware that some people use the two terms interchangeably. It does not really matter for our purposes.

The critical point we want to make is that you need an overarching goal, followed by well-thought-out plans and strategies to reach the final destination that God has planned for you. It will not happen if you sit there and think about it. It will not happen if you only choose to meditate over it. It surely will not happen if you constantly pray about it, but take no action. Nor will it happen if you spend the better part of each day simply praising your God. You need a vision and plans to accomplish it, God will work together with you to do so.

The key is to make a start. Start today and the *corridor principle* will come into operation. The corridor principle states that once you take concrete steps to start something, doors will open for you, one after another, like you are proceeding down a corridor. Then you will begin to see your way clearly. It is a principle used in business, but it can be applied to life in general.

With a Vision, You Look to the Future and Not the Past or Present

Look straight ahead,
and fix your eyes on what lies before you.
Mark out a straight path for your feet;
then stick to the path and stay safe.
Don't get sidetracked;
keep your feet from following evil.

—PROVERBS 4:25–27

A vision will enable you to focus on the future and what you want to achieve in the end. A vision, especially when it is written down and placed in a prominent place to remind you daily, will ensure that you look to the future. You will concentrate on your destination and not your past or your present circumstances. You may be going through a tough time, or your present circumstances may not be encouraging. Therefore, you have a tendency to dwell on your past or present. However, when you do, you are likely to become discouraged. You are likely to fall back on what happened last month, last year, or even a long time ago.

You may have had a terrible childhood. You may have suffered extreme poverty or abuse. You may have a limited education. You may have had a negative experience in a personal relationship, such as the failure of a marriage. Something may have happened in your past that made you think that you are not good enough, that you cannot rise to superstar status. Perhaps it is your physical appearance or another characteristic that makes you think you are not made for greatness.

But once you have a vision, you must not dwell on your past or your present circumstances. Your focus should be only on that vision. It does not mean that you should not learn from your past. Surely you want to learn from previous mistakes and errors in judgment. You should learn from bad experiences in your dealings with certain people, including dear friends and even relatives. You should definitely learn from the past, but you should not dwell on it. Rather, you should look to the future—your destination.

Focusing on your destiny requires commitment and dedication to the cause. That is why you should have your vision written down and placed in a prominent spot in your office, your house, your car, or some other private place that you frequent, so that you will see the vision frequently. You need a constant reminder of your vision. It will keep you focused.

Throughout history, people have overcome their past or present circumstances by forming a vision and focusing on that vision. Through their work they have risen to greatness or superstar status. You can do it too. More importantly, when you are in an ultimate partnership, the power of two will work to help you focus on a vision and then to achieve your destiny.

Jesse Owens was born into poverty in Alabama in 1913. He had a small build, perhaps a below-average physique, and he lacked self-confidence. But his mother instilled in him that God had destined him for greatness. Jesse Owens wondered how that could happen. But one day at a school assembly, one of the most famous athletes in the United States (the fastest runner at the time) gave a presentation which made a deep impression on the young Jesse. Right then and there, Jesse Owens formed a vision of what he wanted to be in life. He told his coach that he had a dream to be the fastest man on earth.

The young boy remained focused on his vision, and he worked hard to achieve it. Jesse Owens rose to become one of the greatest athletes of all time. He fulfilled his dream and became the fastest man on earth. He won four gold medals at the Berlin Olympics in 1936, much to the chagrin and discomfort of Adolf Hitler. Jesse Owens's record in the long jump (broad jump, as it was called then) stood for a quarter of a century. He inspired millions of people in his country and around the world. He used his megastar status to touch lives and help people in the United States and throughout the world. He was duly recognized for his achievements, and he was given numerous awards by countries around the globe. Jesse Owens formed a vision, stayed with it, worked toward it, and he achieved greatness. He died in 1980 and will be remembered as a truly great man.

Nelson Mandela was jailed at Robben Island, near Cape Town in South Africa for some twenty-seven years because of his vision. His dream was to end apartheid and achieve a democratic South Africa. His jailers tried to break his spirit by making him smash rocks for no reason in the blazing African sun. He and others with him were also subjected to additional forms of mistreatment. But Nelson Mandela did not dwell on his circumstances. He looked to the future and remained focused on his vision for his country.

Nelson Mandela played a leading role in ending apartheid, even from prison. He became the first president of a democratic South Africa. Nelson Mandela was not discouraged or deterred by his circumstances in jail. He remained focused on his vision. Today, he is admired the world over and recognized as a moral leader on the global stage. He has received too many international awards and accolades to be counted. He won the Nobel Peace Prize in 1993. Nelson Mandela is one of the greatest human beings who ever lived on this earth.

Similarly, Xanana Gusmao was hunted down as a resistance leader and later jailed in Indonesia for many years. He held on to his vision for a free and independent nation. In 2002, he realized that vision when East Timor became independent from Indonesia and the youngest state to join the United Nations. Xanana Gusmao reluctantly became the first president of that new nation.

When you have a vision, you press on despite what the present circumstances and your past experiences may be telling you. Having a vision ensures that you keep your eye on the prize despite setbacks and disappointments. You hold on to your vision, and you do not give in or give up. You maintain your focus. You must be committed to the vision. Instead of throwing in the towel, when you have a vision you remain focused and continue improving yourself. You know what you want, and your vision tells you that it is out there for you to achieve. You persist. You persevere until you achieve that dream.

Another person who has inspired millions of people around the world is Hicham El Guerrouj, the middle distance runner from Morocco. The men's 1500 meter race was perhaps the most anticipated during the Athens Olympics in 2004. El Guerrouj had dominated the field for almost a decade. He had secured all the major medals except the Olympic gold medal. He failed in both the Atlanta and Sydney Olympic Games, and doubts were beginning to creep into his mind. But El Guerrouj, also known as the "King of the Mile," had a vision to win an Olympic gold medal for himself and his country.

Despite all the setbacks and disappointments, El Guerrouj did not give up on his vision. On the contrary, he persisted. In the most thrilling finish of the Athens Games, El Guerrouj crossed the finish line in the 1500 meter race first, beating a Kenyan champion in the last one hundred meters. The stadium erupted into emotional applause as everyone celebrated with him. The whole world watched on TV.

After winning that gold medal in the 1500 meter race, El Guerrouj remarked "The last few metres I just refused to let him go. I was so desperate for the title that I had to hold on such was the desire in me to win".[1] El Guerrouj proved to those who had written him off that they were completely wrong. In the Athens Olympic Games of 2004, he achieved his vision. A few days later, El Guerrouj also won the 5000-meter gold medal, the first double medal wins in the 1500-meter and 5000-meter races in eighty years.

Before we end this section, let us not forget the many Ethiopian and East African long distance runners who have risen to superstar status. They are people who had to fight abject poverty and living in an environment that discouraged and de-motivated, rather than encouraged and lifted a person up. In the face of seemingly insurmountable obstacles, athletes with a vision and a dream to achieve greatness and break out of poverty and misery have succeeded. They have succeeded because of their vision and focus. They include Haile Gebreselassie and Bikila Abebe. The former won gold medals in both the Atlanta and

Sydney Olympic Games and was a four-time world champion of the 10,000-meter race. The latter won an Olympic gold medal in Rome in 1960, running barefoot. He became the first black African to win an Olympic gold medal.

When asked why he ran barefoot, Bikila Abebe said that he wanted the world to know that his country, Ethiopia, "has always won with determination and heroism." He repeated his extraordinary achievement four years later to win an Olympic gold medal in Tokyo, becoming the first person ever to successfully defend an Olympic marathon win. Bikila Abebe went to Tokyo, after just having surgery, and he was not quite fit for Olympic competition. But he had the vision and determination, and nothing could deter him from achieving that vision.

Maria de Lourdes Mutola of Maputo, Mozambique is another superstar who has inspired people around the world. She had to battle poverty and other forms of adversity, and yet she was able to rise to prominence. She dominated the 800-meter race and capped her accomplishments with a gold medal in the Sydney Olympics in 2000, the first for Mozambique. Maria Mutola has not had it easy, though. She struggled, failing at previous Olympic Games and other competitions. But she had a vision, and despite the setbacks she did not give up. She did not dwell on her past or present circumstances at any time. Instead, she focused on her vision and eventually achieved her dream.

She is universally acclaimed as one of the greatest achievers of our time. She is a shrewd entrepreneur and one of the wealthiest women in the world. She is the first African-American woman to become a billionaire. She is powerful and influential, and in her television talk show she interviews the rich and famous as well as ordinary folk. Her show is watched by more than twenty-one million viewers in the United States alone. She promotes many charitable causes including assistance for those affected by HIV/AIDS in Africa. She is unquestionably a megastar, and her face is recognizable all around the world. We are talking about none other than Oprah Winfrey.

But Oprah did not get to the top without a vision. She started from very humble beginnings. She was born to unmarried, teenage parents. Her family was extremely poor, and she suffered abuse, including sexual abuse, in her childhood years. She proved unsuitable for her first fulltime job as a news reporter, because she had a tendency to become emotional and cry. She was fired from that job. She had many hurdles to overcome, but with determination and patience, Oprah Winfrey rose to greatness. The Oprah Winfrey Show is broadcast to about 100 countries outside the United States, and she has won many awards. Oprah Winfrey had a vision, and she was determined to make it a reality.

Finally, you should be on your guard. Unfortunately, in this world there are people who do not want to see others succeed. These people always have words of discouragement. One of the weapons they use is to constantly remind you of your past and tell you that you cannot make it to the top. These people put labels on you and expect you to live according to those labels. They may even give you nicknames like *dreamer* or *idealist*. These are the same people who place limitations on your future, your dreams, and your goals. They have a victim mentality and are content with a mediocre life.

Avoid such people. They are the vision destroyers. They are the people who will do everything they can to obliterate your vision and leave you stalled. One of the reasons they seek to discourage you is that if you progress, you will expose them. Your advancing in life will show them up, and so they want to keep you down. If you listen to them and do not persist with your vision, the same people will turn around later and tell you how hopeless you are.

So once you have a vision, be on your guard. Avoid those who like to dwell on your past or put you down. Instead, associate with people who share in your dream and encourage you, people who will lift you up when you are feeling discouraged. You need encouraging people around you, not discouraging ones. The whole point of having a vision is to focus on the future, not the past, or even present circumstances. So avoid those people who do not motivate you to focus on the future. There should be no room in your life for them, so shut them out and keep your eye on your vision. It may be far better for you to move to a new environment in which you can associate with encouraging people who inspire you, instead of staying in the same old stale environment and fighting off vision destroyers.

A Vision Requires Goals and Plans to Move You Forward

*The ways in which we will achieve our goals are
bound by context, changing with circumstances
even while remaining steadfast in our commitment
to our vision.*

—NELSON MANDELA

If you live in Europe or the United States and you want to travel to Australia, you have to start making plans in advance. This is for the obvious reason that it will be a long journey, and there are only limited ways by which you can enter Australia. You can either fly or go by sea. There is no other method. Achieving your vision works very much like that. The vision is far ahead in the future, so you need specific goals and plans to help you get to your final destination.

Similarly, if you want to buy a car or a house you have to plan your finances. First, you have to find out how much it will cost you, and then you start to plan how to raise the money. You cannot achieve your vision without various steps to lead you to that vision. You need the steps to lead you there. That is the role of goals and plans. They are the various steps which will lead you to your destiny.

Setting your goals and making plans to achieve your vision does not have to be a complex process. You do not have to engage in an intensive exercise, making up charts, graphs, and the like. You can and you should make it as simple as possible. The purpose is to have a set of navigational tools to lead you to the vision. Whatever goals you set should be for the purpose of your vision only. You are simply defining more clearly the steps that you will be taking to get to that particular destination.

Take the illustration of journeying to Australia from Europe or the United States. You have to plan whether you are going by air or by sea. Everyone knows that even in this day and age it will take you quite some time to get to Australia by sea. So if it is not a leisurely trip for you and time is of some value, you rule out going by sea. The only option left is to fly. Then the next question is whether or not you want to fly there by the most direct route possible. In all likelihood, you will have to stop over somewhere in Asia before you get Down Under. If you want a less strenuous journey, you may decide to have more than one stopover and spend a few days at each place before you get to your destination. The point about all this is that it is very much like having a vision. You need various steps, various goals and plans to achieve the vision. The goals and plans are steps by which to actualize the vision. They may take days or years.

All the people we have discussed in this chapter and in this book who achieved their visions did so by setting goals and making plans. They were all dedicated to their visions. Those in sports had to set up tough training regimens and stick to them. As they went along, they adjusted their goals and plans. Those in politics and other spheres of life also set goals and made revisions as they went along.

The good news is that when you enter into an ultimate partnership, setting goals and making plans for the purposes of achieving your destiny are not things which you do all by yourself. You should remember that your mission was not set by you. It was set by your senior partner in the ultimate partnership, and so it is he who will be guiding you. If you misstep at any time, he will bring you back on the right path. It is in his interest to ensure that you get the right guidance. Psalm 37:23 states that "the steps of the godly are directed by the Lord," and he delights them. Therefore, he will guide you and assist you in this process. In fact, you may not have to do much yourself other than writing down the plans as they are revealed to you. They will be revealed to you in the same manner that your God communicates with you on a regular basis. You do not have to exert enormous amounts of extra energy to receive them. In Proverbs 16:9, the Bible says, "We can make our plans, but the Lord determines our steps."

Summary

In order to achieve your destiny on earth you need a vision to take you there. The vision has to look to the future. It is this overarching aim that will lead you to achieving your mission on earth. Once you have created a vision, you should write it down. You should then focus on it and not be concerned with your past or your present circumstances. You need to be committed and dedicated to achieving that vision and not go about it with a lackadaisical attitude. Even when your present circumstances tell you that you cannot make it, you should focus on the future.

The next action you need is to create goals and plans to help lead you to that vision. Without specific goals and plans you could wander disastrously away from your course. The examples we discussed in this chapter show clearly how many people have achieved their visions despite their past or what seemed to be insurmountable obstacles. People have achieved their destiny in spite of setbacks and disappointments. They achieved their vision because they were focused on it and did not get distracted or discouraged. Visions are achieved in all spheres of human endeavor, not only in particular areas. You, too, can achieve your vision if you follow their examples.

Once you enter into an ultimate partnership, you are not alone. Your senior partner, your own God, will be with you throughout. He will help you to set your vision, and he will also help you set goals and make plans which will lead you to your destiny. It is in God's interest that you succeed and achieve the mission he set for you on this earth. Therefore, it is important to God

to help you set goals and make plans that will realistically lead you to your destiny. It is the power of two in operation.

Power 2 Principles

You must know your mission in life.

Once you know your mission, you need to have a vision.

To accomplish your vision you need goals and plans to guide you.

With the power of two, your God will help you set your vision and develop goals and plans to attain it.

God will always be with you to guide you.

CHAPTER EIGHT

Prosperity and Greatness Will Flow to You

I will bless you and make you famous, and
I will make you a blessing to others.

—GENESIS 12:2

Once you are operating the power of two, the benefits will flow to you. As this book asserted in the beginning, the power of two, or the ultimate partnership, will propel you to greatness, superstar status, or significant achievement. When you have the power of two, your life will no longer be average. You will cease to be mediocre or just surviving from day to day. You will move on to a life of greatness, as we have seen in some of the cases we studied earlier. Once you are operating the power of two, things will never be the same again for you. Not only will you achieve the vision you have set, but you will achieve much more. As long as the ultimate partnership is in operation, there is no limit to the blessings and favor your senior partner, your own God, will bestow on you. As long as you are operating the power of two with him, you can be most certain that you will have an abundance of riches of all sorts, financial, spiritual, emotional, and much more.

Your God will not just bless you. He will make you a blessing to others. It is through you that God will be carrying out his mission on earth. So when he gives you blessings, he will also use you to bless others. Similarly, he may use others who have ultimate partnerships with him to bless you.

We have already seen a number of examples of people who have risen from nothing to superstar status. We will see more in this chapter and the chapters that follow. The starting point is to have the power of two in operation. The rest will follow in due course.

It May Start With Little Things

Unless you are faithful in small matters,
you won't be faithful in large ones.

—LUKE 16:10

One of the books I have in my library is Arundhati Roy's first novel, *The God of Small Things*, written in 1997. I thoroughly enjoyed reading this literary masterpiece. It won the Man Booker Prize the year it was published. It is a story about a small, dysfunctional family in India, but the literary skill of the author makes it read more like thousands of little stories emanating from the book. Overall, it is actually a sad and tragic story.

Your God can also be a god of small things. In fact, it is normal for him to start you with little things, and then as you progress he will provide you with big things. Eventually, you will get to the stage where your blessings will come in buckets. They will continually flow to you and begin to overtake you. That is what is called the overflow.

We discussed in an earlier chapter that when you enter into an ultimate partnership, your God will empower you in general and specifically. He will also provide you with the resources you need to achieve your mission in this world. We have seen how God did it for many people throughout history and in contemporary times. The way it worked in most cases is that when a person entered into an ultimate partnership, God gave them blessings and provisions little by little. Put another way, you will not rise to greatness overnight. It will come incrementally. But as long as you stick to the power of two and are not impatient, your development and rise to superstar status will come along nicely. Your senior partner, your God will deliver on the promises he has made in your ultimate partnership with him, but the benefits will take time to manifest.

THE POWER OF TWO

Jesse Owens and other sports personalities who achieved greatness started out by winning smaller races and competitions. Bishop T. D. Jakes, who is now universally recognized as a powerful man of God, started with a church of only ten members. Similarly, Ray McCauley started his ministry in his parents' living room in Johannesburg. Today, his church membership exceeds 36,000, and his vision is to reach 50,000 in the near future.

I suppose the timeframe depends on each person's mission and how quickly and deeply they develop the ultimate partnership with their God. It may take some people longer than others to see prosperity and greatness flow to them. However long it takes for each individual, it seems clear that the norm is for the greatness to be achieved over time, not overnight. In other words, your own God with whom you operate the power of two is most likely to start out as a god of small blessings. He will shower blessings on you in small measures.

An interesting example is Darlene Zschech of Hillsong Church in Sydney, Australia. Darlene could sing from an early age, but when she joined God in partnership, she began to emerge from obscurity. Her song, *Shout to the Lord*, catapulted her and her worship team to international prominence. Since then, she has composed hit after hit, and Darlene and her team continue to rise. She is a superstar on the international stage, but her prominence has been coming incrementally. It did not happen overnight.

Two South Africans, Rory and Wendy Alec, had a vision to take the gospel to the ends of the world by way of television. They set up God TV about ten years ago and made their first broadcast throughout Europe from their kitchen table in England. It was only two hours long. Next, they increased the show to three hours and then seven hours. Today, God TV broadcasts twenty-four hours a day to Europe, Asia, Africa, and Australia. It has a potential viewing audience of nearly 270 million people in more than 200 nations. Progress came little by little, but today Rory and Wendy have achieved their vision, and they continue to soar to greatness. They touch millions of lives and inspire people around the world.

Megachurches are now springing up all over the world. These are churches with large memberships of thousands of people. Joel Osteen's Lakewood Church in Houston, Texas, Paul Scanlon's Abundant Life Church in Bradford, England, and Brian Houston's Hillsong Church in Sydney are a few examples. But megachurches are not springing up in a few select areas. On the contrary, megachurches are blossoming all over. It is a quiet revival.

For example, Dr. David Oyedepo is the presiding bishop of the Living Faith Church Worldwide (also known as Winners Chapel International). It has a 50,000 seat auditorium, claimed to be the largest in the world, at its headquarters in Lagos, Nigeria. It also has its own university. The church branched out in many African countries. What is common to all these churches is that they started small. They have been building up over years. As the pastors solidified their ultimate partnerships with God, he blessed them and their ministries. Success did not happen immediately.

There may be various reasons why God adopts a gradual approach. We do not really know why, because God's ways are not our ways and his thoughts are not our thoughts (Isaiah 55:8). But we can speculate on some matters. First, perhaps God starts by providing you with blessings in small measures to see whether or not you can be trusted. If you can, then God will let prosperity and greatness flow to you more abundantly. God lifted Saul straightaway to the position of King of Israel, but Saul disappointed God. Samson was another person destined for greatness in the Bible, but he listened to beautiful women rather than God, and he messed up big time.

A second reason why God may start as a god of small blessings is to develop your character. If everything fell into your lap overnight, your character may not develop in a way God would appreciate. This, in turn, would make it difficult for you to achieve your mission on earth. Indeed, if everything fell into your lap, you might be tempted to think that you achieved it through your own efforts, and you might not acknowledge God's part in it. Consequently, by receiving success and provisions in small measures at first, and more importantly, by experiencing setbacks and disappointments, you start to develop a character that relies more heavily on God.

You will learn from your experiences to surrender totally to the power of two. You will not try to rely mostly on the power of one and revert to the power of two only under dire circumstances. Your God does not like that. God does not want you to depend on yourself alone. Rather, he wants you to be totally committed to the operation of the power of two. Therefore, God will start with small victories, prosperity in limited measures, and he will let you experience disappointments and setbacks. It is through some of these experiences that you will learn to rely 100 percent on the power of two. Then God will be in a position to lift you to the next level. That pattern will continue until you achieve abundant prosperity and superstar status. The pattern continues as long as you remain committed to the power of two. You will continue to advance, like some of the examples we have already seen, and do you know what? You will soar to greater heights than you ever imagined. This limitless abundance will be discussed in detail in a later chapter.

By the time Joseph became prime minister in Pharaoh's palace his character was strongly formed, and he was totally committed to a partnership with God. He did not allow any of his earlier setbacks to derail that relationship.

Joyce Meyer, one of the greatest evangelists of our time, has said on many occasions that it took her a long time to reach prominence. She had a bad attitude in the earlier stages of her ministry, and God used many experiences to mold her character and teach her to operate fully on the power of two.

One reason why it is important to have goals and plans for the achievement of your vision is that you will be able to see your development and progress along the way. Maybe this year you will achieve goal number one and cross it off your list. Next year or the year after that, goal number two will be achieved, and then you will cross it off your list. You will see your greatness building over time. It is even possible that when you hit the big time you may not realize it until the accolades start to kick in. You will not notice your success until suddenly your phone starts to ring nonstop, because everyone wants you to be a speaker at their conference or seminar. Or if you are in sports or entertainment, event coordinators will want you to be one of the leading participants. This sudden realization can sneak up on you, because you may not realize the power of the incremental achievements you have been making.

Greatness and Superstar Status Will Come

You should remember at all times that the whole idea of entering into an ultimate partnership with your God is to achieve your destiny on this earth. It is not about your personal ambitions or personal glory. It is about achieving the mission God set for you. That is why you are working together with him to ensure that it is accomplished. You should also bear in mind that your mission is only a part of God's larger plan for life on earth. In other words, your mission is only a small part of God's broader mission. God is working in partnership with you and with millions of others to achieve his larger goal. Your role is to work with him to complete your assignment. But your assignment is part of a bigger picture that God alone can see.

Having said that, you cannot reach your destiny without achieving superstar status in the process. It is you whom people will see carrying out the mission on earth. People will deal face to face with you. For example, Jesus was an evangelist megastar in his time. He still is today. But he was merely fulfilling his mission on earth. He was doing what God sent him here to do. Moses rose to greatness, but he was simply the instrument God used to liberate his people from Egypt. The same can be said of many others. Gideon liberated the Israelites from the Midianites. Nehemiah rebuilt the wall of Jerusalem. Joseph saved God's people from famine. The apostle Paul spread the gospel to the gentiles and beyond. In fact, Paul wrote a big chunk of the New Testament, and today he is one of the most cited writers by Christians, but he was just carrying out his mission.

In contemporary times, God works in the same way. Greatness will come to you because of the unmerited favor your God bestows on you. He will do it out of love for you and commitment to you. Because of the central role you play in the ultimate partnership, superstar status will flow to you. You may be humble, shy, or self-effacing, or you may not like publicity, but once the vision takes off, it takes you with it. The ultimate partnership will drive developments and achievements and not you alone. Remember, it is the power of two and not the power of one. God's favor will come mightily upon you, and it will propel you to greatness (2 Corinthians 12:9).

So greatness will come as you carry out your mission. It will come because you are doing the will of God, not following your personal ambition. Superstar status is available to all, to anyone who is willing to enter into an ultimate partnership with God and operate within it faithfully. Greatness is available to you and to me. It is available to people in the business world, in the military, in service organizations, in sports, and in entertainment. Superstar status can be achieved in any line of work by anyone, as long as they are operating the power of two. It is not only for people who are in the ministry. Anyone can do it. All you need is to commit yourself totally to the power of two, and then the rest will follow. It may take time, but eventually your greatness will start to reveal itself. You will not need to announce it. It will manifest itself for all to see that you have indeed risen to prominence, and you are on your way to greatness. That is when your telephone will start to ring almost nonstop. That is also when your email will be full, because people will desperately want to contact you.

Prosperity and Other Blessings Will Follow

> *The Lord protects them and keeps them alive.*
> *He gives them prosperity and rescues them*
> *from their enemies.*
>
> —PSALM 41:2

It should also be emphasized that God will look at your total situation and empower and bless you accordingly. He will not just dwell on one single mission. For example, you will not have the energy and enthusiasm to accomplish much if you are in poor health. More specifically, you cannot excel in sports if your health is not good. The long and short of it is God will bless you abundantly. If you are in an ultimate partnership with him, you will not only achieve greatness in your immediate mission, but your God will also shower blessings on every aspect of your life. He will grant you the total package, and not just one element of it (2 Corinthians 9:8). We will briefly look at some of God's major blessings next.

Blessings of Good Health

Good health is one of the things we take for granted. For some of us, we have been enjoying good health for such a long time that we begin to forget that this is not something that happens by chance, but rather it is a blessing from God. Everyone on earth needs good health. Without it, your life would be a misery. Without good health, your vision, goals, and plans would remain on paper. You would not be able to implement them. Therefore, good health is critical to your very existence on this earth. When you have good health, you can then carry out your mission on earth.

Unfortunately, many of us take good health for granted. People who live in developed countries with advanced healthcare have a tendency to think that health is not something to be particularly concerned about, because a doctor is just around the corner. I say this because of my own experience living in Australia. It is a big mistake to adopt that attitude. It is when we become complacent and something suddenly hits us, then we wake up.

Recently, my wife suffered a disc collapse. She had to be flown from Addis Ababa, Ethiopia to Johannesburg, South Africa for surgery, because medical facilities in Addis Ababa leave much to be desired. The operation was successful, but she had to remain at home for months recovering from it. She could only move around with the help of a walking stick, and even then she could only walk short distances. Further, she had to sit in an orthopedic chair. After sitting for just a few hours at a time, she had to rest her back by lying down on one side and then the other side.

My wife is an economist, and she was used to working fulltime from Monday to Friday. She was not careless about her health, but that experience made her realize the importance of good health and why she should not take it for granted. It taught me the same lesson. Interestingly, my wife's experience had an impact on many of her colleagues and friends who have since come to realize that one should not take good health for granted, especially as one gets older.

Sadly, when I hear ministers and evangelists preach these days on God's blessings, they often do not say anything at all about good health. They tend to dwell on other blessings, like financial prosperity. However, good health is one of the key blessings that you obtain when you enter into an ultimate partnership. God wants to see you in good health, so that you concentrate on the assignment he has given you instead of spending much of your time and resources going to doctors. As a matter of fact, God may grant you more than just good health (Psalm 103:3; John 1:2). He may grant you excellent health, because once you are fully committed to the power of two, it is his will to give you much more that you desire. You may ask for good health, but in his grace, God may grant you excellent health.

Blessings with Relationships

Have you ever come across somebody who draws people in? On the other hand, do you know somebody who repels people?

The person who draws people in to him or her may be able to hold on to relationships even after moving to a different town, city, or country. I know one such person. That person is my wife. She simply draws people to her wherever she goes without having to do anything. People love her and want to be around her. When my wife had the operation I talked about earlier, the number of visits and phone calls we received was incredible. My wife is a blessing to many people, and many people are a blessing to her.

The other scenario is a person who repels people. He or she is always alone, isolated. This person lacks joy and cheerfulness, and friends do not surround him or her. A person like this withdraws from society and becomes miserable.

Relationships are important to us in life. From when we are born until when we pass on, we will experience many relationships. We have relationships with siblings, spouses, children, and parents. We have relationships in grammar school, college, the workplace, church, and a number of other places. Relationships are important to human living, and therefore it is a big advantage to be blessed with relationships, so that in whatever situation you find yourself, you are not alone. This blessing will ensure not only that you have abundant relationships, but also that you have more positive relationships than toxic ones.

When you enter into an ultimate partnership with God, this is one of the blessings he will grant you. Your God will bless the relationships you form. In fact, he will lead you to people and bring people into your life. From your spouse to your children, your parents to your business associates, God will bless you and the people connected with you, so that you will have positive and fruitful relationships. People around you will see you in a favorable light. In other words, when you are operating the power of two, the hand of God will be on you, and it will influence and impact you wherever you go. The hand of God in your life will show up in the relationships you form. God will cause the people around you to give you favor in everything you do. With God on your side, you will be a blessing to people, and people will be a blessing to you.

Mother Teresa of Calcutta (1910 – 1997) is an instructive example. Born of diminutive stature and already working for God in India, she was given a specific mission by God. It was a mission within a mission to proclaim his love to humanity to the poorest of the poor. Mother Teresa responded to that call, and she rose to greatness. She became a bright, shining star for the whole world to see. She touched and inspired millions of lives around the globe. In her own words:

By blood, I am an Albanian. By citizenship, an Indian.
By faith, I am a Catholic nun.
As to my calling, I belong to the world.
As to my heart, I belong entirely to the Heart of Jesus.[1]

At the time of her death, Mother Teresa's Sisters had nearly 4,000 members, and she had established 610 foundations in 123 countries. In 1979, she was honored with the Nobel Peace Prize. In October of 2003, Pope John Paul II beatified her, meaning that she will be proclaimed a saint at some future time. Mother Teresa of Calcutta rose to greatness when she and God joined in the power of two. She became a colossus on the world stage by mothering the poor and showing love, compassion, kindness, humility, and understanding. She was truly great.

Financial Prosperity

These days we hear a lot about financial prosperity. People talk about it as if it were an isolated blessing. But God does not work like that. If you are in an ultimate partnership with him, your God will grant you financial prosperity, no doubt. But you will be receiving larger and more extensive blessings than financial prosperity (Deuteronomy 28:11).

I do not want to give the mistaken impression that financial prosperity is something that God gives in isolation. That is not true! I do not want to contribute to that wrong impression, so I will not dwell on this topic. All that I want to say is that when you are in an ultimate partnership with God, he will grant you financial prosperity. It is only one part of the total package of blessings God will grant you. God will not grant you financial prosperity and leave your health in poor shape. In a similar vein, God will not grant you financial prosperity to the exclusion of your relationships. If that were to happen, you would find yourself leading a life of isolation, or you would spend all your wealth dealing with toxic relationships.

So the point I am making is that financial prosperity will come, but it will not come in isolation. The case of Mother Teresa of Calcutta shows that by virtue of your calling, financial prosperity may not be a big issue in your life. In her case, God blessed her abundantly with understanding, compassion, kindness, and generosity of spirit. Today, she is on her way to becoming a saint. For Mother Teresa it was not about financial prosperity. Instead, it was about giving love to others.

Victories over Enemies

Do you have enemies? If not, you are quite lucky and the most blessed person on earth. Jesus had enemies, plenty of them in fact. Moses had enemies. Abraham had enemies and so did Joseph. We also know that the apostle Paul in the New Testament had enemies. In fact, all the great men and women of the Bible had enemies. I know I have enemies, and those who are true to themselves know that they also have enemies. It is a fact of life. You do not have to do anything to collect them. They just develop. Enemies emerge out of nowhere.

For example, as soon as Nehemiah returned from exile to rebuild the wall of Jerusalem, some ferocious and trenchant enemies sprang up against him (Nehemiah 2:9; 10; 19). It is a human condition that as long as we live on this earth, we will have enemies. So we better be realistic and learn how to deal with them.

When you are in an ultimate partnership, you can be most certain that you will have scores of enemies. Why? Because when you are oper-ating the power of two, you will rise to superstar status. The favor of God will ensure that you enjoy all manner of blessings, blessings in your health, your marriage, your relationships, financial prosperity and the like. This will without a doubt attract enemies. There will be jealousy and envy. People will start talking behind your back, and they will create rumors about you. Some people will go out of their way to remind you of your past and how you were nobody when they knew you.

Enemies will come, and Satan will have a fertile ground on which to operate. He will have willing and loyal accomplices to try to destabi-lize you. Your enemies will try everything they can to distract you and derail you from achieving your mission.

So it is to be expected that as you rise to greatness enemies will emerge to destroy your vision, your mission, and your goals and plans. Whether you like it or not, you will have to go to battle. You will be drawn into battle by your enemies through persecution and other devious tactics. They want to turn your attention to battle so that your focus will shift from away from your vision. As it is commonly said, your enemies like to bring down the tall poppy. That is you. When you were struggling they were nowhere to be found, but now that you have achieved success, they want to destroy you.

The good news is that when you enter into an ultimate partnership you do not need to lose sleep over enemies, because you will not be on your own. The enemies will come, and they will engage you in battles, whether you like it or not. But your own God will fight your battles for you. One of the main benefits of the ultimate partnership is that God will be with you at all times. God has said specifically that the battles will be his, not yours. In Exodus 14:14, Moses told the Israelites, "The Lord himself will fight for you. You won't have to lift a finger in your defense."

Therefore, when the enemies come, your God will go into battle for you. He will win those battles for you, and you will enjoy the victories. God himself has said that no weapon formed against you will succeed and anyone who manufactures lies against you will be duly punished (Isaiah 54:17).

Winning victories over enemies and living a triumphant life is one of the major benefits of operating the power of two. If you try to engage your enemies on your own, you could spend a lifetime in endless battles, or your enemies could simply overpower you. You should not underestimate the power of your enemies. They can derail your vision, and they may destroy you altogether. But when you are in the ultimate partnership or a power of two, you know that you are fully covered. It will not deter your enemies from trying to bring you down, but you are assured of victory.

Many Never Make It

Lots of people limit their possibilities
by giving up easily. Never tell yourself,
this is too much for me.

—Norman Vincent Peale

I am weary, O God; I am weary and worn out, O God.

—Proverbs 30:1

As you read this book, you may think that I am making it sound too easy. Yes, it is easy. It is not difficult to rise to greatness, but it is not something you can do on your own. If you are able to reach superstar status through the power of one, it will not last long, or you will not attain ultimate fulfillment, or both. The amount of time and resources you will employ to fight enemies alone is enough to take away your joy and inner peace. But when you are operating the power of two, things are easier, because you have a divine power, a higher power, working together with you. God will take care of a lot of things on your behalf. That is what makes the operation of the ultimate partnership so simple. You only need to enter into it and be fully committed to it. The greatness, prosperity, and other blessings will then flow to you. They will be yours.

But let me also emphasize that many people have not been able to make it. Just look around you and you will see people who showed great promise some years back. They may have been people in sports, in entertainment, in universities, or in business. Today they are nowhere to be found. As a matter of fact, many of them have taken their dreams to their graves. They had visions, but they did not pursue them or bring them into reality. They ignored the instruction of Jesus in Matthew 5:15 and hid their lights instead of letting them shine brightly.

The cemeteries are littered with shattered dreams, dreams that remained in people's heads or dreams that sprouted but soon withered away. Those people did not make it, because they relied exclusively on the power of one. They may have entered into the power of two, but fell by the wayside because they were not committed to the ultimate partnership. Perhaps once they started to receive the benefits of the partnership, they decided to do it on their own. When that happens, God also backs off. God will not allow the relationship to be one-sided. Once you decide not to abide by the terms and obligations of the ultimate partnership, God will withdraw from it and terminate the agreement. At that point, what seemed like a promising vision loses steam, and people simply fade away.

Do you remember King Saul in the Bible? That is what happened to him. Do you also remember King Solomon, the wisest and wealthiest man in the Bible? God blessed him mightily, and yet he stopped abiding by the terms of the ultimate partnership. God consequently became angry with him and decided to take away the kingdom from his heirs (1 Kings 11:9–13). Do you remember Samson? He was more interested in beautiful ladies and entertaining crowds than keeping a close relationship with God (Judges 13–16), so God withdrew from the partnership.

The same thing happens today. When you enter into the power of two, God will bless you. But once you decide to end the partnership, God will also withdraw from you and leave you alone. It is meant to be a partnership of two and not a one-person operation. Once you leave it, the partnership ceases to operate, and you lose all the benefits you have derived from that partnership.

Summary

When you enter into an ultimate partnership, God will bless you. He will grant you his favor, and it will reflect in every relationship you form and in everything that you do. It is in your mission that your superstar status will immediately show. Once you are working together with God and his favor is on you, you will rise to greatness in carrying out your mission. It is in the process of achieving your destiny that your greatness will emerge. What will actually propel you to superstar status is the carrying out of your mission on earth. God wants you to do this for him, and therefore he will help you excel. One day when you are heading to eternity, you will look back with pride and satisfaction and say, mission accomplished! Your rise to greatness is a consequence of achieving the mission God gave you.

When the power of two is in operation, God will grant you a total package of blessings. Not only will you receive significant achievement in the mission he has set for you, but you will also receive great blessings and benefits in all other areas of your life. The blessings will show in your relationships, your health, your finances, and in victories over your enemies.

These days some people have a tendency to overemphasize financial prosperity. Sure, your own God will grant you financial prosperity. He does not want to see you living in poverty. But financial prosperity is just one element of the total package of blessings you will receive from the ultimate partnership. Blessings and favor will flow to you in all areas of your life, as long as you are committed to the ultimate partnership. The blessings may start in small measures, but with time they will multiply and allow you to blossom. You should constantly bear in mind that once you end the partnership, your blessings and greatness will also end, because your relationship with God is meant to be a power of two, not a power of one. You should also remember that the blessings you receive are not for you alone. God will use you to be a blessing to others, just as he did with Abraham.

Power 2 Principles

When you are operating the power of two, God will grant you his favor, and you will receive a package of blessings.

The blessings may start in small measures, but with time they will increase.

You will achieve greatness through the mission God has given you. It is in that area that your superstar status will be revealed.

As long as you stay committed to the power of two, your blessings will multiply.

If you end the ultimate partnership, you will lose its benefits.

CHAPTER NINE

Reinvest in the Partnership

For God is the one who gives seed to the farmer and then bread to eat. In the same way, he will give you many opportunities to do good, and he will produce a great harvest of generosity in you.

—2 Corinthians 9:10

If you are in business and you want the business to expand, you have to reinvest in it regularly. In an everyday partnership, if you want your partnership to grow, you have to keep putting effort into it. By doing this you will ensure that the business becomes sustainable. It will grow and expand and before you know it, you will have a large and profitable business.

The opposite is also true. If you just withdraw profits from the business and you do not replenish it, the business will start to shrink, and before you know it, will have to fold and close up shop.

Personally, I love investing. I learned the principles of investing while I was in Australia. I have investments in shares. (I invest in the stock market, but I do not play the stock market! They are two different things. I do the former, but I abhor the latter.) I also invest in real estate at home and overseas, and I invest in other assets. I am a strong believer in investing, whether for the short term, medium term, or long term. My belief in investing extends beyond money and other assets. I also believe in investing in time, energy, and relationships. Therefore,

I do not waste time or energy on unproductive ventures. My mind is strategic, and I invest strategically. I acquired my skills in investing over a period of time. I learned a lot from reading investment and finance books and magazines. I attended seminars and listened to tapes. I did not become an investor overnight. I invested my time, energy, and resources into learning to become a strategic investor.

One of the important elements of investing I learned was how reinvesting can make a significant impact on one's investment portfolio. In particular, I learned about Dividend Reinvestment Plans (or DRPs for short). These are created by major companies for their shareholders. A Dividend Reinvestment Plan is very simple. Instead of receiving cash dividends or profits on your shares from the company, you can opt to have those cash dividends automatically reinvested into the company to buy more shares. This is beneficial to both the company and the investor. It is beneficial to the company, because it does not have to pay out cash. Instead, it can use the cash for further business development. It is also beneficial to the shareholder, because he or she acquires more shares in the company at a discounted rate. In DRPs, the shares are sold to the shareholder at a reduced rate, so they are cheaper than buying them directly on the stock market.

When I first discovered DRPs, I just loved the concept, and I still love it. I have it for all the companies in my share portfolio that offer it as an option. Since I began this form of reinvesting, I have seen the number of my shares in those companies increase markedly without having to put any additional capital into them. Moreover, the price of some of those shares has gone so high that it would have been difficult for me to purchase them on the stock market myself. The DRPs ensure that every time a company declares dividends, mine is used to purchase more shares for me. Of course, this is optional. Whenever I desperately need cash, I can vary the terms of my DRPs and receive cash dividends instead, either wholly or partially. I do not know who invented the concept of DRPs, but it is a great way to expand your investment portfolio without having to inject further capital. In other words, it is a pain-free way to grow your investment portfolio so that it will be more profitable in the future.

The same principle applies to the ultimate partnership. In order for it to be sustainable in the first place, you should reinvest in it. As you put more into it, it will get to the stage where it expands appreciably. You remember we said in the last chapter that the way the power of two works is that your own God will most probably start as a god of small things. He will start by blessing you in small measures to see if you can be trusted. Once he is satisfied that you can be trusted with small things, he will then move you to the next level. When you start receiving blessings in small measures, one of the things you should do is reinvest some of the blessings back into your partnership. As your blessings increase, so should the size and frequency of your reinvestment into the partnership. The more you reinvest in the partnership, the more blessings will flow to you.

The Golden Rule: Give to Your God First

Put some of the first produce from each harvest
into a basket and bring it to the place the Lord
your God chooses for his name to be honored.

—DEUTERONOMY 26:2

One of the golden rules of investing I learned a long time ago came from Robert T. Kiyosaki's books, particularly *Rich Dad, Poor Dad* and *The Cashflow Quandrant*. The golden rule says that you should always pay yourself first. I employed this golden rule for years, but it was when I did not know God. It was when I did not know of the power of two. When you are in an ultimate partnership, you cannot pay yourself first. You are a junior partner in that relationship, and you rely heavily on your senior partner, your God, for his favor and grace. It is through his extra power, his higher power, that you will rise to greatness. It is through the ultimate partnership that your blessings of health, financial prosperity, and victories over enemies will flow. Therefore, you cannot pay yourself first. Instead, you have to give to your God first.

In 2 Corinthians 8:5, the first action of the Christians in Macedonia was to give to God. God is the senior partner, and so you should give to him first. He is the one who empowers you to achieve, and he is the one who gives you the resources you need to operate on earth. God should be the first to see the profits. If you pay yourself first, it means that you are placing yourself as the senior partner; it means that you are valuing yourself more highly than your God, and it is something that God will not appreciate. Proverbs 3:9–10 says that you should honor God with the best part of everything you own, and then he will reward you with an overflow. In some older translations, it refers to the first, not the best. In Malachi 3:10, God actually challenges us to bring him tithes, and then we will see the result. God says in that passage, "I will pour out a blessing so great you won't have enough room to take it in! Try it! Let me prove it to you!"

How do you give to your God? Some people like to spend time debating how much should be given to God. What I say to you is that whenever you receive income, set aside a portion to give to God as soon as possible. Once you have the profit, do not hesitate to give it to God. It would be a mistake to hold onto the money and to try to make more before you give a portion to God. Do you know why? It is through the ultimate partnership that you will become more profitable, and so that should be your absolute priority. Do not fall into the trap of keeping money in the bank or investing it in short term investments. You will make more of a profit in the future if you give God his due.

Act with enthusiasm. Anytime you have the means, give to God first. Once you are in an ultimate partnership with God, you will know how to give to him. You may give to a church or a God-centered activity. God may even ask you to give his portion to a particular person or organization. The fact is that once you are operating within the power of two and you are in regular communication with your God, he will tell you where you should send his portion. In many cases it will be your local church or a recognized charity.

I recently saw a documentary on Evander "The Real Deal" Holyfield, the first and only four-time boxing heavyweight champion of the world. He stated in the documentary that it has always been his policy to give the first 10 percent of his earnings to God. He did so by giving it to his local church. When you consider that as a world champion Holyfield's earnings per fight were in the millions of dollars, the amount he gave to God first would have been quite substantial. His practice of giving to God first is quite separate from the numerous charitable activities in which the former champion boxer has been actively involved.

I believe a number of Christians give a fixed percentage of their earnings to God first. The actual percentage may vary from person to person, and because it is a very private matter, we will never know. The most important thing is that once a person is in an ultimate partnership with God, he or she should give to God first.

An important principle you should keep in mind when applying this golden rule is that giving should not be influenced by taxes or other considerations that will give you a personal advantage. In some countries there are significant tax benefits to giving money to specified charities like churches. When you are giving to God first, you should not be influenced by tax considerations. In other words, you should not give to God first simply because you know that you will get a significant portion back from the government. Nor should the amount that you give be influenced by tax considerations. If there are any tax advantages associated with giving to God first, let them be secondary to your giving. Don't let taxes drive you to give to God. If you do that, it means that in actual fact you are giving to the tax department first and not God first. Tax breaks should not be the first thing on your mind when you give. To avoid this problem, it is better to give to God first and receive nothing at all in return.

Second Rule: Contribute More Generously

Carry out a random act of kindness,
with no expectation of reward,
safe in the knowledge that one day
someone might do the same for you.

—Princess Diana

It is not how much we do,
but how much we put in the doing.

It is not how much we give
but how much love we put in the giving.

—MOTHER TERESA OF CALCUTTA

Giving to your God first is mandatory. In addition to that, you should also develop the habit of giving generously to humanity. By doing this, you are indirectly contributing to the ultimate partnership, because you are doing something of which God approves and encourages. God loves his people on earth, and your direct calling may not be like that of Mother Teresa of Calcutta, who specialized in bringing assistance to fellow human beings. But nevertheless, God wants you to be a blessing to others. So when God blesses you, he wants you to be a blessing to others and for others to be a blessing to you. When you are in an ultimate partnership with God, he may use you as a conduit to reach other people. He may use you to bless others. In 2 Corinthians 8 we are told that after the Christians had first given to God, they gave generously to the assistance of others.

Therefore, you should make it a point to contribute generously to the lives of others. It does not require much. You can do any number of things to help people around you. If you have money, let your money talk. If you do not have money, but you have some special skill, gift, or talent, use it to contribute to the lives of others. You may decide to go and help with the work of a charity on weekends. You may decide to give talks to motivate children in orphanages. If you have a skill in sports, you may decide to go and pass that skill on to disadvantaged children. There are many other things you can do. Jesus told his apostles in Matthew 10:8 "Give as freely as you have received."

However, as the common saying goes, charity begins at home. Start with your own family and friends and then gradually expand. Sometimes, all that you have to do is smile and encourage others. It makes their day. Perhaps you can just be a good listener to someone who needs a shoulder to cry on. Make yourself available to them, and be the person to whom they can go to blow off steam. Become your own version of Mother Teresa.

Diana, Princess of Wales started from humble beginnings, even though she had royal blood. She was a kindergarten teacher before she married the future king of England. She soon rose to greatness and eventually became a megastar on the world stage. She captured the imagination of the world with her beauty and style. She emerged from the background of the future king to captivate the world. She helped hundreds of charities during her short life. She devoted time to help homeless children, children with disabilities, children affected by HIV and AIDS, and she led a campaign to ban the manufacture and use of landmines. She was the patron of over one hundred charities during her lifetime. She died tragically in a car accident in France in 1997.

The world loved Diana, and everywhere she went, people could not get enough of her. The world loved Diana, because Diana loved the world. She loved and cared for people. She gave freely of her love, her time, her compassion, and her kindness. She once said, "Helping people in need is a good and essential part of my life, a kind of destiny."[1] Princess Diana was so loved that she was given nicknames like "Princess Di," "Queen of Hearts," and the "People's Princess." Positive and encouraging people attract other positive and encouraging people. Princess Diana met Mother Teresa in the Bronx, New York just months before Diana's passing. Her tragic death shocked everyone, and the whole world mourned her.

Bill Gates is an outstanding person of our times. He has become famous around the world, not only for his company, Microsoft, but also for being the richest man on earth. Bill Gates has added to his fame by being one of the greatest philanthropists in history. Through the Bill and Melinda Gates Foundation, he has given away billions of dollars to various causes around the globe. Bill Gates is using his wealth to support such causes as a worldwide infant vaccination program, research on malaria, a fight against tuberculosis, and a comprehensive attack on HIV/AIDS. In 2005 alone, the Bill and Melinda Gates Foundation pledged more than one billion dollars for global health. Bill Gates is truly great as an inventor, an innovative thinker, an entrepreneur, and a person who really cares about his fellow human beings. He is a blessing to humanity, especially the poor and disadvantaged.

Throughout history, people have given generously to those in need, and people continue to do so today. There are many organizations that provide generously for the benefit of others. There are numerous foundations for this purpose in countries all around the world. It is better to join them and be part of their contribution, rather than sitting on the sidelines and thinking of making money only for yourself. People who give generously to the lives of others tend to live more abundant lives than people who do not. Those who have a generous spirit, good cheer, and a positive outlook on life bring positive energy to everything they do and everywhere they go.

Today, celebrities contribute their time, money, and skills to benefit others. This is not the place to create a who's who list of generous givers, but here are a few contemporaries: Michael Jordan (a variety of charitable organizations for youth); Tiger Woods (charities for youth); Bono of U2 (elimination of Third World debt, global poverty, and other causes); Oprah Winfrey (diverse causes); and Sir Bob Geldof (elimination of Third World debt and global poverty). The list goes on and on. Generous people can be found in every nation of the world. Special recognition was given to Bono and Bill and Melinda Gates for their magnificent contribution to charitable causes in recent times. *Time* Magazine voted the three of them Persons of the Year in 2005.

Let me challenge you. At the end of each month, take stock. Make a list of the people you have helped in the month, whether you helped them with money, business, sports, work, problems, or whatever. When you help others, your senior partner in the ultimate partnership recognizes your work. He will continue to bless you and increase your blessings. The Bible teaches us the following, "Give generously, for your gifts will return to you later" (Ecclesiastes 11:1).

Summary

When you are in an ultimate partnership, you should continue to reinvest in that relationship. Like business partnership, you need to reinvest so that it will grow and expand with time. This is how your blessings will continue to flow to the point of overtaking you.

The golden rule is that you should give to your God first. He is the source of your power, your resources, your protection, and everything else, so he should get priority. The second rule is that you should contribute to humanity. You should contribute to the lives of people around you. Your God wants to use you as a conduit to bless others and to use others as a conduit to bless you. Don't forget that your mission is only a small part of God's broader mission on earth. You are important, and your mission is important. But as far as God is concerned, it is connected with other missions which are equally important to him. Therefore, your God wants you to be a blessing to others and for others to be a blessing to you. You can achieve this by contributing generously to the lives of others. You do not have to only contribute money or material assets. You can give love, compassion, and kindness. A simple smile, hug, or handshake is a gift. Just give it freely!

Power 2 Principles

In order to sustain the ultimate partnership and allow it to grow and expand, you must reinvest in it on a continual basis.

The golden rule is to give to your God first.

As you reinvest and the partnership grows, your blessings will also multiply.

The second rule is that you should give to humanity. Your God wants you to be a blessing to others and others to be a blessing to you.

|||||||||||||||||||||||||||||||||||||||||||||||||||||||||||||||||||||||||||||||||||||||||||||||||||||||||||||||||||||||||||||||||||||||||||||||||||||||||||||||||||||||||||||||||||||||||||||||||||||

CHAPTER TEN

Recession Will Come

The recession we had to have.

—PAUL KEATING,

FORMER PRIME MINISTER OF AUSTRALIA

One of the most controversial statements ever made in Australian political and economic history was, "The recession we had to have." When Paul Keating spoke those words, he was Treasurer of Australia, which is the equivalent of Minister of Finance or Minister for Economic Planning in other countries. In the late 1980s, Australia enjoyed an economic boom. However, in the early 1990s, the country went into a recession. Housing interest rates reached 17 percent, and life was tough throughout the country. I know, because I experienced it myself.

There was a general outrage in the country when Keating argued that the recession was necessary to correct structural weaknesses in the Australian economy. Attacks came from all sides, and nasty jokes against him mushroomed. One of the more popular jokes ran something like this: The definition of a recession is when your neighbor loses his or her job. The definition of a depression is when you lose your job.

Paul Keating is a passionate man. He is a person of strong convictions—especially for a politician. He has a forceful personality. He is not a person easily swayed by public complaints and populist actions. Despite the mounting public anger, Paul Keating refused to budge and allowed the recession to bite, as he pressed ahead with his reforms to the Australian economy. The remarkable thing is that despite the nasty recession (which could have been ameliorated), Paul Keating's party went on to win the next election and the one after that. Paul Keating rose to become Prime Minister of Australia. The country has enjoyed economic prosperity for the last decade or so, and many, if not all, Australians maintain that Australia's prosperity today is due largely to the strong stand Paul Keating took in the early 1990s. Australia is reaping the benefits of the "recession we had to have," they argue.

This is an instructive illustration. In life, periods of difficulty or trouble will come. Some will be brief; others will last for awhile and may pose serious challenges to you and your vision for the future. If you are in business, then you already know what I am talking about. In business, a recession is something that comes every now and again. An astute businessperson learns to weather the storm, because just as day comes after night, better economic times will definitely follow bad times. Business is cyclical.

In life, it is more or less the same. Everyone goes through tough times every now and again. They can come in different shades and forms for different people, but they will come for each and every one of us. I can say with absolute confidence that no one on this earth escapes a bad patch, a horrible season, or a valley. So we have to learn to go through those times and not allow ourselves to be overwhelmed by them when our turn comes.

It is Only a Passing Phase

Obstacles don't have to stop you. If you run into
a wall, don't turn around and give up. Figure out
how to climb it, go through it, or work around it.
—MICHAEL JORDAN

The Bible teaches us that life is made up of seasons, and there is a time for everything (Ecclesiastes 3:1). Unfortunately, there is a time for valleys, recessions, turbulence, and bad patches. It does not matter what you call them, they surely will come, and you won't need anyone to tell you that they have arrived.

The first thing to learn about bad patches is that they will definitely come. The form they take for you may be different from your neighbor. For example, if you are a church minister, you may experience a period when your sermons don't seem to have the same impact as they did previously. Or maybe your church congregation has stagnated after a period of rapid growth. Worse, you may experience a shrinking of your numbers.

If you are a sports person, you may find that suddenly you are not as fast as you used to be, or you can no longer attain a score you previously reached. If you are a creative person, such as a songwriter or an author, you may find yourself experiencing long periods of writer's block. Maybe you are coming up with work that you think is masterful, but everyone else sees it as below your previous standards. For politicians, bad patches are easy to spot. When your approval ratings plummet, you know without a doubt you are in trouble.

I have heard some people say that the only place on earth where there is absolute peace and tranquility and where you will not experience any turbulence is in the cemetery. I wonder whether this view is entirely correct, because I have seen with my own eyes how the peace and tranquility of the dead have been shattered. In many developing countries grave robbery is not uncommon at all, and the dead in some cemeteries have found themselves and their resting places rudely disturbed and violated. Even in developed countries I have read about graves in cemeteries being desecrated. Of course, this is unacceptable and also illegal, but it does happen. It is a fact of life—or rather the afterlife. The point is that there is really no place on this earth where troubles do not come. The only place where it is guaranteed that there will be no turbulence, recession, or valleys is heaven.

Secondly, a bad patch is only a passing phase. It is only for a season. Sometimes, it may seem like there's no end to your troubles. If you have lost your job and you have not obtained another one yet, you may think there is no end to your troubles. If you are in business and your bottom line does not seem to be improving, you may wonder when the turnaround will be coming. Similarly, if you are being threatened with the loss of your house or car due to repossession by a bank or finance company, you may think that your valley is the deepest that ever existed.

The nature and length of troubling times will vary from person to person, but one thing remains the same, they are just passing phases. No matter how deep and rugged your valley seems to you, it will end. Psalm 23:4 talks about walking through the valley of the shadow of death. It does not talk about sitting there with your arms crossed, feeling sorry for yourself. Nor does it talk of brooding over your loss or setback. On the contrary, it talks about going through it—walking through and not remaining there.

Not long ago, I visited Rhema Church in Johannesburg, and I heard Pastor Ray McCauley preach that when you are in a valley, you should not build a hotel there. Nor should you erect a tent and make yourself comfortable there. Ray McCauley also said that the worst thing you can do is to start to boast that your accommodation in the valley is the nicest. You are not supposed to remain in the valley for a long period of time. Definitely do not take up residence there. On the contrary, you are supposed to be passing through. You should be on the move in that place, not building a home there.

An illuminating contemporary example is that of John Winston Howard. Between the 1980s and the 1990s, his political career went through a turbulent period. Things were quite humiliating for him, and cartoonists, humorists, and media commentators had a field day with his difficulties. He became leader of the Liberal Party, and thus the leader of the opposition in the Australian Federal Parliament. But he was thrown out of that post twice, because his colleagues did not think that he was prime minister material. Many people would have been discouraged by those experiences and would have given up completely, but John Howard was determined, and he did not allow his valley experiences to defeat him. When he regained the leadership of his party and became the leader of the opposition in the Australian Parliament again, he described himself as "Lazarus with a triple bypass." John Howard did not allow his setbacks and failures to overwhelm him. In March

1996, John Howard won a landslide victory and became Australia's 25th Prime Minister. He has since gone on to make history by becoming Australia's second longest serving prime minister after Sir Robert Menzies.

The third lesson to learn from difficult times is you will eventually emerge from that bad patch. No matter how difficult the experience, no matter how deep and rough the valley, you will emerge from it. You will reach a mountaintop after your valley experience, and you will rise higher than ever before. On the other hand, to paraphrase Ray McCauley, if you take up residence in the valley and start to boast that you have the most prestigious address in the place, then you will finish down there.

The story of Job in the Bible is perhaps the most dramatic and most instructive on experiencing a valley (a nasty one at that) and emerging from it. Job was a great man, and he was wealthy. He had an ultimate partnership with God, and God was very pleased with him. God himself described Job as "the finest man in all the earth—a man of complete integrity" (Job 1:8).

However, one day things started to fall apart around him. Bad news came with each hour. First, he lost all his possessions. Next, he lost his children. It was a case of bad news on top of bad news—all in one day! Then, Job was afflicted with a terrible case of boils. His wife could not take their suffering anymore, and she asked her husband to abandon God and curse him. But Job rebuked his wife and refused to abandon God (Job 2:8–10). In other words, Job maintained steadfastly to the ultimate partnership, even in the face of a desperate situation.

Job's turbulence went on for quite some time. According to the Bible, Job's life became impossible. It was a living nightmare. He lost his reputation and credibility in the eyes of his community. For a person who was a great man and had an impeccable character, it was a severe blow. Don't forget that Job did not move to a new town. His fall from grace was witnessed by the community where he had always lived, and surely his fall was the talk of the town. But Job did not waver or give up on God. Eventually, just as the calamity had come, it evaporated. All the pain and anguish disappeared literally overnight. God then blessed

Job even more. He rose to even greater heights and became wealthier than he was before he found himself in difficult times.

Mention should also be made of the Apostle Paul in the New Testament. His valleys and recessions seemed to have no end. The man simply went through a gamut of troubles for Jesus. Paul experienced a shipwreck, jailing, stoning, attempted assassination of him, hunger, pain, misunderstandings, misfortunes, snake attack, etc. But Paul never gave up—he took it all in his stride and persisted with his mission (Acts 20:19–24).

In sum, recessions, valleys, and turbulence will come to you, but they will only last a season. No matter how long they might seem, they will not last forever. They have a time limit, an expiration date that will definitely come up. You have to hang in there and press on with your vision and your mission. The Bible teaches in Psalm 30:5 that you may experience weeping all night, but joy will surely come with the morning.

Recessions, Valleys, and the Power of Two

When you go through deep waters and great trouble,
I will be with you. When you go through rivers of difficulty,
you will not drown! When you walk through the fire of oppression,
you will not be burned up; the flames will not consume you.

—ISAIAH 43:2

The question you may now be anxious to ask is will a person who is operating a power of two still experience recessions, valleys, or turbulence in life? The short answer is yes, and I will explain why here.

The first lesson we learned was that bad patches will most definitely come to you and me in this life. If you are operating a power of one, when your recession hits, you will be on your own. There will be no one to fall back on. You will have to figure out all by yourself what has happened to you, how long it will last, and if you will ever get out of it. If you are operating a power of one, you will have to marshal all your energy, resources, and time into dealing with the difficulty. Mentally, that can prove to be exhausting. Emotionally, it will be very taxing. Physically, it will be draining.

Losing sleep? There is no doubt that you will lose sleep, lots of sleep in fact, as you go through a valley or a recession. It is something to be dreaded, but unfortunately it cannot be avoided.

On the other hand, when you are operating a power of two, the situation will be totally different. I am not suggesting that it will be a piece of cake for you. I am not suggesting that at all. If it was easy, it would not be a valley for you. The main difference between someone who is operating the power of two and someone who is not is in the obvious fact that in the former, the person is not alone. In fact, the person has a powerful ally, a powerful companion who will be going through the valley together with him or her. You should remember at all times that in the power of two the powers of you and your higher power are combined. You are operating together, rather than operating two separate powers. So actually you will be going through the valley together with your higher power. You will be shielded from the full force or impact of the recession.

In contrast to someone who is operating on a power of one, a person who is in the power of two is given cover and shield. He or she will not be going through the valley alone but accompanied by a superior force, a higher power. That is why in Psalm 23:4 it says, "I will not be afraid, for you are close beside me." In some translations, it says, "I will not be afraid, for you are close beside me, guarding, guiding all the way." [1] So that is a key difference between a person with the power of two and someone without it.

The second message that comes from that psalm is that your God, your own God, will be comforting you as you go through the pain and agony of turbulent times. So he is not only there to give you companionship and courage, he also protects you and when the pain hits. God provides you comfort and solace. Above all, your senior partner in the power of two will give you hope. In Hosea 2:15, God himself says that he will transform the valley of troubles "into a gateway of hope."

You should bear in mind that a valley or recession may be brought on by God himself for a specific purpose. God may want to use challenges to correct deficiencies or weaknesses in your character, very much like Paul Keating did with "the recession we had to have" in

Australia. Maybe some attitudes or habits you have developed are hindering you from achieving the mission God has set for you. That is frustrating for God, and he will engineer a recession in your life to give you the opportunity to iron out those deficiencies.

In 1 Peter 1:7 we are taught that trials and challenges test our faith in God and purify us for the next level in our development. You may be on your way to greatness, and then suddenly you find that you have stagnated, and you do not know why. If you are operating the power of two, you need to ask your senior partner what has gone wrong, and surely he will tell you.

Joyce Meyer has said on many occasions that once she learned what God's plans were for her, she could not wait to rise to the top. She was in a hurry and wanted everything to happen quickly. She had a bad attitude at various times. Consequently, God allowed bad patches to hit her, and God used them to mold her character and personality and ultimately enable her achieve her mission. Joyce Meyer has since risen to greatness in Christian ministry.

Sometimes the problem may not be bad attitudes or habits. God might have taken you on a path to achieve greatness as far as your present circumstances would allow. There may be a gap somewhere. It could be in your skills, training, or experience, in your emotional state, or in some other area of your life. In other words, you have been doing the right thing, but you have risen as high as you can go, and you are far from achieving your destiny. You may even be a superstar already, but you need some additional power to sustain it or rise further. God may use a recession to reveal to you that you have stagnated or stalled, because you do not have what it takes to propel yourself to the next level.

You may be doing fine where you are now, but God wants to move you to a higher level. In that case, God will use the opportunity of a recession to train you further, to empower you to do what is required to move to the next level. God uses that opportunity to refine and mold you, to prepare you for the next stage on your path to destiny. God will be with you throughout the challenging experience. He will order your steps as you pass through the valley and then lead you up the other side of the mountain. Before long, you will see yourself rising to the top again.

God used the various valley experiences Joseph went through to prepare him for the post of Prime Minister of Egypt. Each experience toughened and matured him. Joseph was a dreamer, and perhaps he was naïve in telling his brothers about his dreams when he was young. By the time they met again in Egypt, Joseph's experiences had molded him into a different character. The next time around, Joseph did not rush to reveal himself to his brothers. He made sure that he had all of them together, and then he went about it in a way that did not drive his brothers away from him.

So God may let a recession occur as part of his own plan to prepare you for the next level in your development and help you achieve your destiny. You remember we said earlier that your God could be a god of small things. If you are taking a long time to master what he has entrusted to you in small measures, you could experience a longer period of recession than most.

When Nelson Mandela went to jail, he was a militant freedom fighter, and he was willing to use violent means to overthrow the apartheid regime of South Africa. His spirit was not broken after twenty-seven years of valley experience, and he had not given up on his vision, but instead formed a new character. Today, Nelson Mandela commands moral authority all over the world. Even the President of the United States, the Prime Minister of the United Kingdom, and the Secretary-General of the United Nations do not command the same level of moral authority as Nelson Mandela. God turned Nelson Mandela into what he is today through his valley experience in jail on Robben Island.

Don't Allow Yourself to be Sucked Into a Depression

Do not abandon yourselves to despair.
We are the Easter people and hallelujah is our song.
—POPE JOHN PAUL II

We said before that many people do not make it to their destinies. They do not make it, because they allow the turbulence to overwhelm them.

They end up in a life of mediocrity. For some of them, their dreams or visions were not even given the opportunity to come out of their heads. Others talked a lot but did nothing. Still others started along their paths to destiny with great enthusiasm, but when the recession came, they buckled. For many people, their dreams and visions end up being buried with them. The cemeteries have become repositories for unrealized dreams.

When a person is operating on the power of one, this can easily happen to them. But when a person is operating the power of two, they can also fall by the wayside. They will fall when they abandon the ultimate partnership and start to question the existence or faithfulness of their God. Once they withdraw from the ultimate partnership, God will let them go. He will welcome them back if they decide to come back, but as long as they choose to be on their own, they will find that the valley experience will take longer. They may decide to take up residence there.

The story of Samson in the Bible is a very good example of this (Judges 13–16). Samson was destined for greatness, and God was with him from birth. But Samson became more interested in beautiful ladies and public entertainment than having a partnership with God. As we know, Samson did not live up to his promise, and his life ended tragically.

A person who has an ultimate partnership with God may also stagnate if they decide not to follow through with the orders of God. For example, if a person in an ultimate partnership stops giving to God his first earnings or stops helping others, that person could find himself or herself stagnating. God may still be with him or her, but a rise to greatness may suffer serious setbacks. This may explain why there are so many people around who showed early promise but soon faded away from the scene. There was no extra power to sustain it. They were like shooting stars that showed up in the skies, bedazzled everyone, and soon burned out.

A valley, by definition, has mountains or hills on all sides. Thus, when you go down into a valley from one mountainside, you can expect to emerge at another. There are many valleys in on earth, but the scariest is believed to be the appropriately named Death Valley in California. It is one of the hottest places on the entire earth, and long stretches of sand dunes make the place look like the Sahara Desert. Movies like the *Return of the Jedi* were partially filmed in the Death Valley. But even this desolate place has been conquered by man, and it is now a major tourist attraction, though not for the fainthearted.

A geographical depression, on the other hand is, a crater which is deep and can stretch over a large distance. In layperson's terms, a depression is a mighty hole that is deep and can also be long. There are some well-known depressions in the world including Asal in Djibouti (156 meters below sea level), Turpan Depression in China (154 meters below sea level), Qattara Depression in Egypt (133 meters below sea level), Karagiye Depression in Kazakhstan (132 meters below sea level), and Denakil Depression in Ethiopia (125 meters below sea level). To give you a better understanding of what a depression looks like, let us look briefly at the last one, the Denakil Depression in Ethiopia. It is also called the Dallol Depression. It is in a desert, and it is one of the lowest points on earth not covered by water, making it a true depression of the earth. It is extremely hot, and temperatures can get as high as sixty-three degrees Celsius or 145 degrees Fahrenheit. Earth tremors occur with alarming frequency, and there are also a few active volcanoes. Would you want to live in a place like this?

So we get metaphors for valleys and depressions from these geographical formations. Obviously, a valley is challenging but can be overcome. When you move from one mountain down into the valley, you know that you can get out at the other end, though it may take you some time to do so. But a depression is not a place you want to be in. It is desolate, fearful, and can suck the life out of you. Indeed, depressions like the Dallol and the Qattara in Egypt are not inhabited by humans. That is why the term *economic depression* is reserved for the worst economic scenario possible. Throughout history, there have not been many economic depressions, though economic recessions are much more common. In fact, the last great economic depression occurred in the 1930s. Countries can handle recessions, but they fear an economic depression, because once it grips a national economy, it spins like a whirlwind, and the consequences can be quite disastrous. It is from that same metaphor that we now have such terms as *mental depression, emotional depression*, and *psychological depression*.

The point is, when your personal recession comes, don't let it develop into a depression. Once you get into the latter, it will spin you around; your life will turn into a nightmare; and if you are not lucky, you may never recover from it. My advice is simple: handle a recession with care, and avoid a depression at all costs. When you are operating the power of one and you have no anchor in your life, you have to be extremely careful how you handle a recession, especially when it seems protracted. If you mishandle it, you could easily find yourself in a depression. That is when people who once showed great promise drop by the wayside. People who allow themselves to be overwhelmed by recessions end up in depressions, and then they give up on life altogether. When an aircraft experiences severe turbulence and the pilot loses control, the result is usually a crash. Similarly, if you do not have a firm anchor in your life and you experience severe turbulence, you could lose control, and then what started as a recession turns into a depression.

Perhaps the most famous book ever to come out of Africa is Chinua Achebe's *Things Fall Apart* (1958). More than eight million copies have been printed, and the book has been translated into more than fifty languages. Achebe's book actually took its title from a poem by the famous Irish poet and writer, W.B. Yeats. He wrote in one of his poems published in 1921 that, "things fall apart, the centre cannot hold" and anarchy was unleashed on earth. This is an apt description of what can happen to a person who experiences turbulence in life and then loses control and goes into a depression.

How the Power of Two Can Work for You

I command you—be strong and courageous!
Do not be afraid or discouraged.
For the Lord Your God is with you wherever you go.

—Joshua 1:9

When you are operating the power of two, it is unlikely that your situation will slip from a recession into a depression. Sure, your recession could be deep and protracted, but your senior partner—your higher power—will not allow you to slip past him into a depression. There are two reasons for this. First, God has promised that under no circumstances will he allow you to be challenged beyond what you can handle (1 Corinthians 10:13). Your God knows your limits, and he will not let you endure more pain and hardship than you can take. He knows your limits, because he created you. If you are in the ultimate partnership with him, he will continue to be aware of your limitations. The confidence in God to shield us through valleys and turbulence is expressed in this way:

> We are pressed on every side by troubles
> but we are not crushed and broken.
> We are perplexed, but we don't give up and quit.
> We are hunted down, but God never abandons us.
> We get knocked down, but we get up again and keep going.
>
> —2 Corinthians 4:8–9

Therefore, regardless of how your recession comes, if you are operating the power of two, your God will shield you. You may be stretched to the limits, but he will ensure that you are not stretched past your tolerance level, because he does not want you to slip into a depression. Even if it is not God who brought you into that valley, God will protect you, because you are in an ultimate partnership with him. This is one of his obligations in the agreement.

Secondly, if you are in the ultimate partnership and you have been following the advice and recommendations in this book, you have identified a vision that you have written down. You also have specific goals and plans to help you achieve your mission. When you are following your goals and plans, you are not likely to become so overwhelmed by a recession that you lose control and slip into a depression. Do you know why? Because your vision will always guide you. You will be focusing on the future. As the years go by, you will see whether or not you are heading toward your vision. You will continually monitor and evaluate your goals and plans, and you will see areas that need review, revision, and adaptation. You will make the necessary changes as time goes on. Sometimes, you may need to change your vision entirely, because you realize you got it wrong or you overemphasized one aspect of it. Therefore, when you have goals and plans to help you complete your mission, you will know how to make adjustments when you hit a recession.

The other side of the coin is that through your goals and plans you will know when you do not need to make major changes. You will recognize that in certain situations it is just a matter of remaining focused on your vision and staying the course. In those situations, the bad patch will eventually subside, and you will continue on the path to your destiny.

For example, sometimes when a plane hits turbulence, the pilot informs the passengers to keep their seatbelts fastened and stay in their seats. The pilot is more vigilant, but the flight path does not change. After awhile, the turbulence ends, and the flight continues as if nothing happened. I have personally experienced this many times.

Regardless of the origin of your turbulence, as long as you remain in the ultimate partnership with God and do not give up, your God will restore to you whatever you lose during the period of the recession. More importantly, your God will propel you to greater heights and shower you with greater blessings. There is a purpose for going through a difficult period, and once you have passed the test, you will be rewarded. Even if the recession is the work of the enemy, God will turn it to your favor and bless you for remaining steadfast in the partnership and learning the lessons that God wanted you to learn from the experience (Genesis 50:20). The story of Job discussed earlier is our best education on this subject.

Summary

Recession or turbulence will surely come to you in this life. It is inevitable. Troubles may come because an enemy sees that you are on the rise to greatness and wants to do everything to undermine you and stop you from achieving your destiny. God himself may bring turbulence into your life, or allow it to come to you, to help develop your character. God may use bad patches to help you mature and prepare you to launch into bigger and better things in life. When you are operating the power of two, you will not be going through those valleys alone. God will be with you throughout the difficult times and shield you from slipping into a depression.

Moreover, your goals and plans will keep you focused on your vision. They will ensure that you look to the future and don't dwell on your present circumstances, however difficult they may be. Therefore, even when recession hits, you are not likely to be so distracted or derailed. You may go through some tough times, but because you have a vision, goals, and plans, you will not suddenly stop moving toward your destiny. Rather, you will review and adjust the goals and plans as necessary. The most important thing is that you remain focused on your vision.

The other point to make is that because you are in the ultimate partnership, you will not only emerge victorious, but like Job in the Bible, you will rise to greater heights in whatever you do. Prosperity will flow to you in even greater abundance.

Power 2 Principles

In life, there will be times when you experience periods of turbulence. They are inescapable.

Difficult times are only a passing phase in your life, but you need an anchor to keep you from falling apart and ending up in a depression.

If you are operating the power of two, your God will shield you. He will use your experience to prepare you for the next level on your path.

With a power of two, you will emerge victorious from the valley. You will then rise to greater heights and receive more blessings.

CHAPTER ELEVEN

You Need Determination and Patience

Life was not meant to be easy!

—Malcolm Fraser,

former Prime Minister of Australia

Many of us will have to pass through the valley
of the shadow of death again and again before
we reach the mountaintops of our desires.

—Nelson Mandela

I have heard that remaining at the top is harder than getting there. The reality is that in order to achieve your destiny in life, you will need a lot of determination and patience. Unfortunately, life is not easy. I was in Australia when Prime Minister Fraser made the remark quoted above. I still remember the verbal attacks that were unleashed on him, particularly by his political opponents. Malcolm Fraser came from a background of wealth and privilege in Australia, and so his political opponents argued that he was only concerned with people from privileged backgrounds and not the disadvantaged in society. The poor felt that they could not expect much assistance from a leader who talked like that. Malcolm Fraser has not been able to shake off the badge of dishonor brought on by his ill-timed observation.

Having experienced some five decades of life myself, on four different continents, I salute Malcolm Fraser for speaking the truth. Life is not easy at all. Even with advanced educational qualifications, life can be tough. I have seen it in the lives of many people. Some people may be fortunate to have had a reasonably good start in life with the help of their parents, but even then life is hardly a smooth ride. The stark reality is that life is full of twists and turns, and you need determination and patience, not only to get to the top, but to remain there. You need determination to enable you rise higher and higher and obtain fulfillment in life. I said at the beginning of this book that there are people who have made it to the top, and yet they can't sleep at night. They have no peace and fulfillment. There is something missing in their lives. They still need the power of two, despite the achievements they have made.

Whether you are just starting on the path to your destiny, whether you are already far along the path, or whether you are very close to achieving your destiny, you will need a lot of determination and patience to arrive at your final destination. You need these two important human characteristics, because without them, you could easily become diverted from your course. Without determination and patience, you could fall by the wayside when challenges hit. In fact, you could be cruising along nicely, and then out of nowhere you are hit by a tsunami, a hurricane, a typhoon, a tornado, an earthquake or some other mighty disaster. You might have passed through valleys in the past, and you were beginning to think that you were through the difficult times. Suddenly, the storm hits and threatens not only to take you off the path of your destiny, but to destroy you completely.

Unfortunately, life has a habit of doing this, and therefore you need determination and patience. It does not matter what your station in life or where you are at present along the path to your destiny. Don't tell me that you are too old. You need determination and patience as long as you are in this life. There is no question about this. Those who did not have these important human characteristics have fallen by the wayside. Some people who started very well in life have since faded from the limelight. They failed to achieve their missions in life. There are those also who rose to greatness or even superstar status, but they did not last long. When the storms of life hit them, they did not have the determination and patience to carry on. They forgot what Sir Winston Churchill said about never giving in, and they crumbled. Yes, these people are like boxers who go into the ring and display impressive skills. They quickly get ahead in points, but once they're hit by a big punch, they drop to the floor and do not get up. They lack determination and patience, and so they get knocked out instead of knocked down.

You Need Determination in Everything and for Everything

Fight one more round. When your feet are so tired that you have to shuffle back to the center of the ring, fight one more round. When your arms are so tired that you can hardly lift your hands to come on guard, fight one more round. When your nose is bleeding and your eyes are black, and you are so tired that you wish your opponent would crack you one on the jaw and put you to sleep, fight one more round—remembering that the man who always fights one more round is never whipped.

—JAMES J. CORBETT

You need determination in all aspects of your life. You need determination from the beginning to the end of everything you do, if you are to achieve greatness. From the moment you get an idea in your mind until it comes to fruition, you need determination to make it happen. Determination is necessary to ensure that your mind is filled only with positive and inspiring thoughts. That is a start. Next, you need determination to ensure that negative and discouraging ideas, suggestions, and thoughts do not make their way into your mind and cause you confusion. Then, your positive and inspiring thoughts will translate into positive and inspiring language, ideas, attitudes, and actions. To be a great champion, you need persistence and patience. You have to continue fighting until you actually win. This applies to all aspects of your life, not only the major challenges you face.

In particular, you need determination to come up with your vision, mission, goals, and plans. There will always be things competing for your time and attention. It is a tough world in which we live. Sometimes, you find yourself so busy that you hardly have time to work on your mission. Therefore, determination is required to ensure that you do not give up on your ultimate goal. Further, you need determination to ensure that you faithfully implement your goals and plans and do not deviate from the course you have charted.

So let me emphasize that you need determination in all aspects of life, if you are to achieve superstar status. Nothing great in life comes easily. You have to work at it, chip away at it slowly but surely. I have often said that to achieve most goals in life, you have to work at them little by little. You need determination to propel you from one small achievement to the next. Then, you find you will move on to bigger achievements. Through it all, you need to be fiercely determined and never give up.

However, it is when you experience difficulties that you need a lot more determination. That is when you find your path littered with obstacles and hurdles. I have already gone over the causes of recession and turbulent times, and so I will not repeat the discussion here. The important thing to remember is that once you go through a storm, there will be bigger and better rewards on the other side of it. Yes, once you have gone through the valley, you will rise to a higher status. The period of recession prepared you to handle bigger challenges and more difficult situations. Put another way, you will be conditioned for higher office, for greater glory, and for superstar status. You need those valleys to prepare you, but if you do not have the necessary determination to weather the storms, you will fall by the wayside, and your dreams will evaporate. That is how some people end up taking up residence in the valley, instead of just passing through and making it to the mountaintop. It is how dreams and visions end up being buried with their dreamers.

The same goes for the great storms of life. They can hit you at any time, but life has a habit of reserving them for those individuals who are heading for greater glory. In other words, the valleys and recessions prepare you to rise to greatness, but the hurricanes of life can prepare you for even greater achievement. You need more serious challenges and attacks to prepare your character for greater achievement, for megastar status. Therefore, when these disasters hit you, you should understand that all you have to do is to withstand them and not give up or give in. Those challenges are setting you up for better and bigger achievements. Remain firm and steadfast, even if the tsunami is destroying everything around you. It is your resilience and fortitude that will see you through.

I can say with confidence, having lived on a number of continents, especially continents that are known for typhoons and other natural disasters, that they are always short-lived. I once experienced a cyclone firsthand when I was in Townsville, North Queensland in Australia. It was devastating, but it was also short-lived. In 2004 and 2005, the world witnessed some of the deadliest natural disasters in history. From the tsunami of southeast Asia to Hurricane Katrina and Hurricane Rita that hit the United States, it was a horrible time in the world. Unfortunately, some of the disasters, especially the tsunami of southeast Asia and Hurricane Katrina, caused extensive damage to property, and many lives were lost. The economic, social, and environmental effects of those natural disasters will be felt for a long time. The devastation is obvious, but the fact remains that the actual duration of the natural disasters were short-lived.

The point I am trying to make here is that every natural disaster has a lifespan, and usually it is short. No natural disaster has continued to rage for a very long time. Even volcanoes explode and spill forth lava, but then they are quiet again. The same principle goes for the disasters of life. They have a limited duration and eventually come to an end. Of course, when they hit us, we have no idea how long they will last or how much devastation they will cause. That is when fear and doubt can set in, but as long as you remain determined and continue on, you will eventually see your storm recede and then disappear. Just as all natural disasters have a limited lifespan, so it is with disasters of life. In order to survive them when they hit, you need determination. Without determination, you will be swept away. These are not trials for the fainthearted. They are reserved for those on their way to true greatness. Those who are able to overcome the big challenges of life are ready to achieve their missions and in so doing become truly great. However, you need bulldog tenacity; you need determination to make it that far.

You Also Need Patience

Be persistent, whether the time is favorable or not.
Patiently correct, rebuke, and encourage
your people with good teaching.

—2 Timothy 4:2

Patience is the flipside of determination. By definition, determination requires that you wait for something, the thing you are determined to achieve. Therefore, you need patience to wait for the outcome. No matter how determined you may be, you must have patience to get to the results of that determination. Sometimes you need little determination, and other times you need a lot of it. In a similar way, sometimes just a little patience is all that is required. In many cases, a lot of patience is necessary to see you through a challenge. It is stating the obvious to say that when the problem is big, a lot more determination is needed, and thus a lot more patience is also required to see you through. When you are passing through a valley, you will need more than just a little patience.

When you are hit by the storms of life, you have to dig deep for determination. Your patience should also have depth, or you are likely to crumble and fall by the wayside. Then you will see your dreams evaporate before your eyes, because you did not have the tenacity and patience to come through a major challenge in your life. That is how many people kill their visions. It is how many people fail to accomplish their mission in life. They finish the course, but they have nothing to show for it, because they never found out why they were put on this earth in the first place.

There is an important aspect of patience that should be highlighted. When you are waiting for something to happen, it is important that you do so with a positive attitude. You are waiting patiently for something to take place, and you are doing so with determination, but the trials and storms are still around you. Your patience will be sorely tested by the storms you face. Your patience may be stretched to the limit. Consequently, you need a positive attitude to see you through.

In other words, there is much more to it than merely waiting patiently for something to occur. If you have negative and discouraging thoughts plaguing you during the period of trial, you could end up developing a negative attitude. Worse, you could become a twisted and nasty person—complaining all the time, being unnecessarily aggressive, and putting off everyone who crosses your path. This in turn affects your relationships and a whole host of other areas. Through your twisted behavior, you announce to the world that you are not coping well with your problems and challenges.

When you have a positive attitude and a cheerful outlook, you ride through your storms without many people noticing at all. In fact, those who know you are going through a storm in your life will come to admire you tremendously. They will see that in the midst of your troubles, you are composed, and you have peace. You will be an inspiration and a blessing to others. Your time of adversity could be a source of inspiration to many, simply through the way you handle your challenges. In sum, your patience and determination should be carried out with a positive attitude.

Some Instructive Examples

Everyone faces challenges in life. You have faced some challenges in your life already, but more are yet to come. That's right, you are not done. I don't have to be a prophet to be able to say this. It is the way life works. You need determination and patience to ride through any challenge, small or large. History teaches us that those who have fortitude and patience never fail. Sure, they went through very trying circumstances, but in the end, they made it. They had some setbacks, but they were only temporary. They came through victoriously as champions and conquerors. There were times when all seemed lost; there were times when it seemed like they had failed; but they never gave up. They did not give in or give up, and in the end they emerged victorious.

There are many such examples. You can find them in all walks of life and in all parts of the world. Some are famous, but there are also many unknown examples of people who overcame great challenges in their lives with determination and patience.

From the Bible

The first illustration is a woman who had a hemorrhage. She had lived with this debilitating and humiliating problem for twelve years (Mark 5:24–34; Luke 8:43–48). She spent all her time and money on doctors, but to no avail. When she learned of Jesus, she was determined to get help and healing from him. She had faith, and she had to do whatever she could to make contact with Jesus. So with determination, this woman pushed her way through the crowds and barely touched the edge of Jesus's robes. The fact that she was able to get close enough to Jesus to touch his clothes showed a high level of persistence. The woman was healed, and her twelve-year problem was solved forever. Jesus wanted to know who had touched him, but even his own disciplines thought he made a ridiculous demand. How could Jesus seriously ask that question in the midst of such a great crowd of people pushing and shoving to get close to him? But Jesus was insistent, and so the woman admitted to being the one who touched his garment. The woman was determined to touch Jesus, and she eventually succeeded and was healed.

The second example is a gentile woman Jesus met when he went north to the region of Tyre. This woman went to Jesus and asked him to cast an evil spirit out of her daughter (Mark 7:24–30; Matthew 15:21–28). Jesus was reluctant, and so the woman pleaded with him and fell at his feet. But Jesus was still not moved. In fact, he said that his mission was primarily to help the Jewish people. However, the woman would not go away. She had guts. She was determined to obtain healing from Jesus for her daughter. Therefore, despite what Jesus said, she pleaded with him to extend his hand of healing to her daughter. Jesus was so impressed with the woman's determination, that he obliged and healed the little girl from a distance. That was persistence in action.

Furthermore, we should not forget Ruth in the Old Testament. She was determined to go with Naomi wherever she went. Ruth's loyalty to Naomi and determination and patience to remain with her took Ruth from Moab to Judah. It was in Judah that Ruth found a husband and started a family. King David and Jesus came from her bloodline (Ruth 1:16–18; 4:17).

Contemporary Examples

Throughout this book we have referred to famous examples of determination and patience. I will add just a few more here, starting with Nelson Mandela. His political opponents locked him up in jail on Robben Island near Cape Town in South Africa for twenty-seven years. He was made to smash rocks in the scorching African sun for no real purpose. There were times his jailers tried to get him to abandon his vision and beliefs, but Nelson Mandela was a man of steel, and he refused to compromise his vision. He suffered greatly, but his spirit was never broken. After twenty-seven years of hard labor, he emerged to become president of a democratic South Africa. Today, he is recognized throughout the world as a leader with moral authority. Through his suffering, Nelson Mandela helped to destroy the pernicious apartheid regime in South Africa. Twenty-seven years is a long time in anyone's book. But you will appreciate the gravity of Nelson Mandela's term even more deeply when it is put into context. The life expectancy in a number of African countries today is about thirty-five years. Nelson Mandela spent twenty-seven years in jail, just because of his vision.

We discussed earlier that Xanana Gusmao fought the Indonesian colonists in the jungles, and later he was jailed for many years. But he had determination and patience, and so he did not give up his vision. He overcame all that the Indonesian authorities threw at him, and eventually he achieved his vision of an independent and democratic East Timor.

There are many similar examples of African, Asian, Caribbean, and

Latin American leaders who defeated colonialism and imperialism and obtained independence for their countries by using determination and patience. Today, Aung San Suu Kyi remains under house arrest in her own country of Myanmar (Burma), and she is not allowed to leave the country. She has suffered untold hardships and restrictions since her party won the general elections in 1990, but the military junta refused to accept the election results and nullified them. Aung San Suu Kyi has been recognized all over the world as a non-violent, pro-democracy activist. She has won many prestigious prizes, including the Nobel Prize for Peace and the Sakharov Prize for Freedom of Thought. She has had many opportunities to give up her vision and compromise with the military, but her unflinching determination and patience keep her going. She has her eyes on her vision, and no amount of suffering and deprivation will discourage her.

Determination and patience apply to all aspects of life. They are not restricted to any particular profession or human endeavor. On the contrary, one needs determination and patience to succeed in any walk of life. In sports, because it is a very public human endeavor, we can see how determination and patience propel people to superstar status. In chapter eight, we discussed how some people overcame adversity to achieve international fame and glory in sports. Their determination and patience enabled them to beat all the odds. In particular, we referred to athletes from eastern Africa who had to battle deep poverty and lack of facilities to break into the international arena and achieve greatness.

In more recent times, Maria de Lourdes Mutola of Mozambique suffered many setbacks and disappointments in her running career, but she did not quit. Her determination and patience eventually led her to win the gold medal, which had previously eluded her, in the women's 800 meter at the Sydney Olympic Games in 2000.

Furthermore, there was high drama in the Olympic stadium at the Athens Olympics in 2004 when Hicham El Guerrouj of Morocco won his first gold medal. The "King of the Mile" had won all the races there were to win in order to establish himself as the world champion, but the Olympic gold medal eluded him. He suffered countless setbacks and disappointments, particularly at the Atlanta and Sydney Games, but he never gave up. His persistence and patience told him to give it one more try at the Athens Olympics. At those Games, not only did he win the gold medal in the men's 1500 meter race, he also won a gold medal in the 5000 meter race, a feat that had not been achieved in eighty years.

The Power of Two and Determination and Patience

God blesses the people who patiently endure testing. Afterward they will receive the crown of life that God has promised to those who love him.

—JAMES 1:12

Whether you have the power of two or not, you are going to need determination and patience to make it to the top and stay there. The difference that the power of two makes is that you will not go through life's challenges alone. Whether they are minor valleys or big storms, when you have the power of two you will face them with inner peace and confidence. You will know that your own God is with you, and he is guiding you and protecting you with every step.

Your God will also help you to maintain determination and patience. On days when you feel like throwing in the towel, your God will grant you new strength and vitality to press ahead. In a boxing contest, it is not the boxer in the ring who throws in the towel. It is kept in the corner by the boxer's trainer. It is the latter who throws in the towel when the boxer cannot take it anymore. When you have the power of two, it is your God who will be keeping your towel, and he won't throw it in and pull you out. With God on your side, you will have patience, because you will know you have to wait for his promises to manifest. It will only be a matter of time, but you have to wait with positive thoughts and attitudes and not allow yourself to worry or complain. In Jeremiah 29:11, God assures you that the plans he has for you are good, and he will not let disaster overwhelm you. His plans are to give you a future full of hope and not defeat.

The most important aspect of all is regular communication with your God. He will be telling you as you go along that he is working on your case, and you do not need to have fear or doubt. From time to time, God will let you know that he is going through the challenges of life with you. The fight is God's, but the victory will be yours to savor. So that is the key difference between someone who has the power of two and someone who does not. A person with the power of two will be able to face life's challenges with confidence, peace, and joy, because he or she knows that God is in control.

Throughout history in most cultures the eagle has been associated with grace, power, and fearlessness. An eagle is not afraid of a storm. It simply soars higher and higher above the tempest. In the Bible, the eagle is mentioned many times. For example, Isaiah 40:31 states:

But those who wait on the Lord will find new strength.
They will fly high on wings like eagles.
They will run and not grow weary.
They will walk and not faint.

If you have the power of two, you will be like an eagle. You will have grace and fearlessness. Specifically, you will not be afraid of a storm, because you know it will allow you to soar higher and higher in due time.

Let me emphasize that it would be a mistake to think that with the power of two a person can avoid life's challenges completely. There is no such thing. God himself has said that he has not promised to help you escape life's challenges. Even Jesus faced challenges throughout his ministry. If you operate with the power of two, you will still face the storms of life, but you will be able to handle them more assuredly. You will have the inner peace and confidence to go through challenges knowing that you are traveling with God. Because there is divine power to shield you, you will be able to weather those storms and challenges with assurance and confidence. Psalm 34:19 states, "The righteous face

many troubles, but the Lord rescues them from each and every one."
(See also Job 5:19.)

Equally important, when it is all over, you will rise to further greatness and superstar status. In other words, the major challenges of life
will prepare you for further achievement and greatness. Challenges and
storms are opportunities for God to test your faith in him. God wants
to make your faith in him solid and unshakable, very much in the same
way that fire is used to test and purify gold (1 Peter 1:7). The God you
serve is the God of the impossible. He can make something happen
when all logic says that it is unattainable. "For nothing is impossible
with God" (Luke 1:37).

God parted the Red Sea; made a virgin conceive and deliver
a son; raised people from the dead; ordered storms to be calm; and
turned dry bones into a formidable army. Consequently, when the
hurricane of life throws you high in the air, God will give you a safe
landing. He will not let you come crashing to your death. He will be
there to stretch out his hands and pick you up. When God operates
within you in the power of two, there is no disaster of life that you
cannot handle (1 John 4:4). The disaster may seem threatening, but
you have something more powerful inside you, and you will overcome
the challenge. God can order the storm to cease when it comes to you.
It may hit everyone around you, but God can order it to leave you
alone. On the other hand, the storm may toss you around, but when
God gives the order, it will obey and become silent (Mark 4:35–41;
Matthew 8:23–27; Luke 8:22–25).

There are scores of examples in the Bible of people who had ultimate partnerships with God and still faced storms in their lives. Those
people had the power of two, and yet they did not escape major challenges. The difference is that God was with them, and he helped them
out of the storms. In the Old Testament we can refer to Daniel. He
experienced his tsunami when he was thrown into the lions den, but
his God shut the lions' mouths. Daniel was determined to always worship and pray to his own God and no other.

Similarly, the three Jewish boys (Shadrach, Meshach and Abednego)
faced their own hurricane of life when they were tied up and thrown

into the burning furnace. God sent a divine being to be with them in the furnace. Their determination not to bow down and worship King Nebuchadnezzar's gold statue triumphed (Daniel 3:19–28).

Another instructive example of determination and patience is David. After being anointed king of Israel, he had to wait for many years and wage several battles before he could take over the leadership of Israel. As a matter of fact, David was anointed three times before he became king over all of Israel (1 Samuel 16; 2 Samuel 2 & 5). God had anointed him, but David still had to overcome numerous challenges to get to the position God had reserved for him.

There are also various examples in the New Testament of determination and patience by people who had the power of two. They suffered many trials and tribulations, but in the end their fortitude and patience ensured that they did not deviate from their visions. Of course, their God helped them along the way. The apostle Paul is perhaps the best illustration. He suffered persecution, whipping, stoning, shipwrecks, a snake attack, robbery, imprisonment, poverty, and other forms of adversity (2 Corinthians 11:22–33). But with unflinching determination and patience he stood firm in his faith and his confidence in Jesus, and he preached the gospel to the gentiles right to the end. He never lost focus.

The Legend of Abraham Lincoln

No discussion on determination and patience would be complete without at least a reference to Abraham Lincoln. He is one of the greatest examples of those two human characteristics, if not the greatest. He experienced great adversity in his lifetime, adversity that would have made many people give up and quit. But Abraham Lincoln's resilience, persistence, and patience knew no bounds. He had unlimited reserves of those qualities, and in the end, they paid off.

He was born in a one-room log cabin on a farm in Kentucky, and his mother died when he was only nine years old. His family was forced out of their home, and so he had to forgo formal education and work to help take care of his family. He decided to educate himself. Failures and setbacks were the norm for Abraham Lincoln rather than the exception. He lost his job and tried to enter law school, but he was not accepted. Nevertheless, he eventually became a lawyer and then entered politics. He failed in business ventures twice, and he was declared bankrupt once. The young lady he was engaged to marry died, and it broke his heart. He also suffered a nervous breakdown on one occasion and was bedridden for six months. He lost eight elections, including failing to become speaker of his state legislature and his first attempt to enter the United States Congress. Several attempts to enter the Senate also met with failure. Despite all these setbacks, Abraham Lincoln never quit. He was determined to win, and the word defeat was not part of his vocabulary. In 1860, he became the sixteenth president of the United States, and to date he remains one of the greatest presidents of that country.

Abraham Lincoln's persistence, bulldog tenacity, and unyielding commitment are legendary. People who suffered only half of the setbacks he endured would have long given up. But from Abraham Lincoln we also learn patience. He was determined and committed to his vision, but he was also patient, and he was never dissuaded by his present or past circumstances. Rather, he always looked to the vision, the dream, the future, and eventually he achieved his vision.

When the legend of Abraham Lincoln is told, one significant aspect is often overlooked. Abraham Lincoln knew God. He believed in God, and more importantly, he depended on God. Although he never joined a church, he regularly attended church while he was president. On March 30, 1863, President Lincoln stated the following in a proclamation declaring a national day of fasting:

Whereas, it is the duty of nations as well as of men to own their dependence upon the overruling power of God, to confess their sins and transgressions, in humble sorrow, yet with assured hope that genuine repentance will lead to mercy and pardon, and to recognize the sublime truth, announced in the Holy Scriptures, and proven by all history, that those nations only are blessed whose God is the Lord.

President Lincoln's speeches are laced with similar expressions of the power of God and the need to be dependent on him. Abraham Lincoln is legendary for his patience, persistence, and tenacity, but he was also dependent on God. Who could have survived the storms of life that Abraham Lincoln endured without God?

Power 2 Principles

Determination and patience are absolutely necessary for you to rise to greatness.

When the storms of life come, you need determination and patience to press ahead to victory.

With the power of two, you will still face challenges in life. You cannot escape them.

Your God will bring you through the storms, and you will overcome challenges and then move forward on the path to your destiny.

CHAPTER TWELVE

Then You Will Rise to Greater Heights and Achieve More Prosperity

*We give great honor to those who endure
under suffering. Job is an example of a man
who endured patiently. From his experience
we see how the Lord's plan finally ended in
good, for he is full of tenderness and mercy.*

—JAMES 5:11

I am sure that you have heard it said many times that the calm follows the storm. After enduring numerous setbacks and failures for decades, Abraham Lincoln rose to become the sixteenth president of the United States. In addition, he won a second term as president. His achievements were many, yet he faced even more challenges as president. He had to go to war to save the United States from collapse when the South tried to break away. With a reservoir of determination and tenacity, he fought the South for four years and won, and slavery came to an end in America. Abraham Lincoln had a vision for a united country and outlined it in the famous Gettysburg Address he gave on November 19, 1863. His leadership shaped the destiny of the United States. From a background of hardship, Abraham Lincoln rose to greater heights, and he became one of the greatest presidents of the United States and one of the most influential people in world history.

John Howard faced many challenges and setbacks in his political career. He lost the leadership of his political party several times and suffered humiliation. He became the butt of jokes, and the cartoonists, in particular, had a field day with him. But John Howard did not give up. His determination and patience paid off handsomely when his party turned to him to rescue them after their preferred leaders could not deliver. "Lazarus with a triple bypass," as he once described himself, rose from the political doldrums to become the twenty-fifth prime minister of Australia. He has since risen to greater heights—he is now the second longest serving prime minister of Australia.

Yes, calm comes after the storm. But when you have the power of two, it is much more than that. I have already said that all natural disasters have a limited time span. So, too, have the disasters and troubles of life. The storms of life operate in a similar way. They have limited spans. You may think that your troubles or challenges do not seem to have an end, but that is in your mind. Your mind is the battlefield. Like all other troubles and challenges, yours have a limited time span. They have an expiration date, and when that date comes, they will simply evaporate. As a matter of fact, storms and other disasters have a tendency to end suddenly. But when you are operating the power of two, you will find that you will overcome the disaster or challenge no matter how fierce. When your resilience and fortitude have held up against the challenge, it will simply disappear. That is when the hurricane of life reaches its due date. It is finished and evaporates into thin air.

However, with the power of two you experience much more than just the calm after the storm. We discussed earlier that after you pass through the valley, you will get to the mountaintop. After the turbulence, your God will ensure that you have a safe landing. After your recession, you will experience growth again. We said that facing life's challenges is a continuous thing. You will not experience one big challenge, and then it is over. Rather, as former Australian prime minister Malcolm Fraser said, "Life was not meant to be easy." Therefore, you will experience many challenges throughout your life.

I remember, when we were in university in the late 1970s in Ghana, a popular slogan used by the student movement in its campaigns against the government for better conditions on the campuses was *aluta continua!* It means: the struggle continues. I later learned that the slogan

THE POWER OF TWO

had its origins in Latin America, where liberation movements used it to motivate themselves during their struggles against colonialism and imperialism. *Aluta continua* on every continent, developed or not. That is why, when you find yourself in the valley of the shadow of death, you should be determined to pass through it. Do not remain stationed there, for it is not a place meant for residence. It is meant for passing through so that you can get to the other side. But if you do not have the power of two, you can easily find yourself remaining in the valley and making it your abode. Then, you have allowed your failure to turn into defeat. You have allowed a temporary setback to be permanent.

We also said that when you overcome your valleys with the power of two, you will reap the rewards. You will rise to greatness and make significant achievements in your life. You will gain success and prosperity in various forms. Your God will bless you and allow you to prosper. You will find yourself on the mountaintop. From there, you can look down into the valley and see that you have come a long way, indeed. You will see that you are definitely on the path to achieving your destiny, though you are not yet there. You will see that you are getting closer and closer to achieving your mission in life.

The pattern is the same with the storms of life. When they are over, your God will bless you even more. When your fortitude and patience have been proven beyond a doubt, when you have kept the faith with your God through it all, you will then rise to even greater heights than before. Your greatness will shine with more glory. Blessings will flow your way. You will become a true superstar, and even a megastar, regardless of your calling, career, industry, or vocation.

The truth is that when you are operating the power of two and remain faithful to your God through any disaster, he will reward you abundantly. In fact, you will experience an overflow of blessings. We said earlier that your God can be a god of small things. The small things train you for bigger things. Therefore, when you pass each test that comes your way, God will promote you to the next stage. Once God can trust you in small things, he will entrust big things to you.

Furthermore, we said that God will take a keen interest in how you handle the challenges of life. Sometimes, he will orchestrate them himself; other times, he will allow them to happen. They are meant to develop your character or provide you greater wisdom and maturity. As the Bible puts it, he wants to make your faith rock-solid and purify you, just as gold is purified through fire (1 Peter 1:7). What you have now may be sufficient for your present circumstances, but to rise to the next level you need a deeper understanding and appreciation of God. You need to be refined and remolded until you are ready for that next step on the path to your destiny. Therefore, he will use various challenges to prepare you for the next level. The greater the challenges, the faster they will help to propel you to prosperity. That is why the Bible enjoins us to count ourselves fortunate when challenges and troubles come our way (James 1:2; 1 Peter 1:6). They are opportunities for us to rise to the next level, to even greater achievement and significance.

When you have overcome the storms of life by keeping the faith, God will shower his blessings on you. You are then at the dawn of superstar status. Throughout the Bible, God demonstrated this principle so clearly and powerfully that we cannot miss the point. Daniel faced his greatest challenge when he was thrown into the den of lions. With God on his side, he overcame that challenge and went on to prosper (Daniel 6). The throwing of Shadrach, Meshach, and Abednego into the burning furnace was tantamount to their facing a hurricane of life. When they emerged victorious from it, they were promoted to higher offices in the land of Babylon (Daniel 3:30). In other words, Daniel and the three Jewish boys rose to greater heights and prosperity after they had passed major tests in life.

A very illuminating example is Job. He was a significant person in his community when he was hit by a cyclone of life. In a matter of days, Job was reduced from being a wealthy and powerful man to having a life of wretchedness and disease. His life was thrown into total turmoil, and his bearings were severely disrupted. But Job's anchor was his God, and through it all he remained faithful to the Lord. His patience and fortitude were just as solid as his confidence in God. Job was, without a doubt, buffeted by a mighty storm of life. His wife gave up, but Job was resilient and resisted her suggestion to do likewise. God himself challenged Job, and after he passed the test, he was richly blessed. Prosperity flowed his way, and he became wealthier than he was before he was hit with challenges. He was also blessed with a long and happy life thereafter.

Even Jesus faced major challenges during his ministry. Specifically, he defeated Satan after he was baptized. He emerged from the wilderness and returned to Galilee filled with the power of the Holy Spirit. He was then ready to take on the religious leaders and rise to greatness.

Furthermore, God has made it clear that if you lose something in the course of facing your challenges, he will make sure that he restores it to you. A natural disaster can leave lasting damage. For example, the effects of Hurricane Katrina will be felt in the United States for years to come. Katrina did catastrophic damage to the coastlines of Louisiana, Mississippi, and Alabama. It is recorded as the worst hurricane in United States history, having killed some 1,417 people and caused damage to the tune of eighty billion dollars. Then Hurricane Rita arrived, and finally Hurricane Wilma, the strongest ever recorded hurricane on the Atlantic coast. In all, the United States experienced a total of fifteen hurricanes in 2005 alone, and the damage that was caused was massive.

The point of this digression is that the damage caused by a natural disaster can be extensive and costly. Indeed, some of the damage may be permanent. In contrast, when you have an ultimate partnership, your God will make sure that your temporary setback does not result in permanent loss or damage. Therefore, when the storm is over, he does not only bring you calm and peace, he restores everything that you have lost. He will then proceed to do more—much more—for you. You will be overwhelmed with blessings. God will grant you an overflow of greatness, prosperity, and achievement. 1 Peter 5:10 states:

In his kindness God called you to his eternal glory by means of Jesus Christ. After you have suffered a little while, he will restore, support, and strengthe you, and he will place you on a firm foundation.

Joyce Meyer is one of the greatest evangelists of our time. Her preaching is broadcast weekly on TV to some two billion people in about two-thirds of the countries in the world. She touches lives throughout the ends of the earth. She is, without a doubt, a megastar on the world stage and is fulfilling the mission God gave her. However, Joyce Meyer had to overcome many struggles and challenges in her life to rise to true greatness.

Similarly, Bishop T. D. Jakes is universally recognized as a mighty man of God. He had to overcome a myriad of challenges and storms to rise to the top.

There are numerous other examples around the world. People have risen to greatness after overcoming incredible challenges in their lives. This is not limited to working in a church. Rather, examples can be found in all walks of life, in all human endeavors.

Finally, when you overcome your challenges, you will find peace and fulfillment. You will be full of joy and good cheer. It is human nature to experience some destabilization when mighty storms come. Your peace and fulfillment may be disturbed. But once you overcome the challenges and you are back on your path to achieving your destiny, peace and fulfillment will return. In fact, God will grant you his peace, that extraordinary peace and fulfillment that human beings cannot attain by themselves (Philippians 4:7).

CHAPTER THIRTEEN

Keep Reinforcing and Renewing the Partnership

Instead of shame and dishonor, you will inherit a double portion of prosperity and everlasting joy.

—Isaiah 61:7

I promised you at the beginning of this book that it would change your life. I have shared with you the ideas and principles of the power of two, or the ultimate partnership. I have supported the points I made with actual experiences, historical and contemporary. I have also shared my own experiences with you. Now is the time to apply the ideas and principles of the power of two. If you have not already started, go back to the beginning of this book and start putting the ideas and principles into practice. Start today—don't delay any longer! You will find your mission in life. With your vision, goals, and plans, and all that you have learned in this book, you will rise to greatness, superstar status, or even higher. Remember that more challenges and storms may come to you. Continue to renew your partnership with God, and you will always come out on top. Make this book your companion on your journey, and you will find true greatness and fulfillment at last!

Finally, celebrate each day that you have on this earth. You have a limited time here, and each day presents you with opportunities to carry out your mission. Celebrate each day and begin it with confidence, peace, and joy. Do not wait for another day!

Notes

CHAPTER 2

1. At one stage, Tyson became a Muslim, but not much was heard about this after a short while.
2. *USA Today*, June 3, 2005.
3. Ibid.

CHAPTER 7

1. *Middle East Online*, August 25, 2004.

CHAPTER 8

1. The Vatican, "Mother Teresa of Calcutta (1910–1997, biography)," Vatican: the Holy See, http://www.vatican.va/news.

CHAPTER 9

1. QuotationsBook, s.v. "Diana, Princess of Wales," quote, http://quotationsbook.com/quote/35961">Helping.

CHAPTER 10

1. Parents Resource Bible; The Living Bible.